G R JORDAN

Our Gated Community

A Highland and Islands Detective Thriller

First published by Carpetless Publishing 2021

First edition

ISBN: 978-1-914073-10-6

This book was professionally typeset on Reedsy.
Find out more at reedsy.com

Contents

Foreword

This story is set on the Monach Islands and various locations around Glasgow. Although incorporating known cities, towns and villages, note that all persons and specific places are fictional and not to be confused with actual buildings and structures which have been used as an inspirational canvas to tell a completely fictional story.

Acknowledgement

To Susan, Harold, Jean and Rosemary for your work in bringing this novel to completion, your time and effort is deeply appreciated.

Novels by G R Jordan

The Highlands and Islands Detective series (Crime)

1. Water's Edge
2. The Bothy
3. The Horror Weekend
4. The Small Ferry
5. Dead at Third Man
6. The Pirate Club
7. A Personal Agenda
8. A Just Punishment
9. The Numerous Deaths of Santa Claus
10. Our Gated Community
11. The Satchel

The Contessa Munroe Mysteries (Cozy Mystery)

1. Corpse Reviver

The Patrick Smythe Series (Crime)

1. The Disappearance of Russell Hadleigh
2. The Graves of Calgary Bay

Chapter 1

Ross tried to stop himself from being sick as the boat lurched up and down in the choppy sea. Although the trip would be a short one, and hopefully, the body found in the town square would be a routine death, he was already regretting his bosses being away on a conference. Left with Stewart to hold the fort unless something juicy came in—Macleod's words, not his own—Ross had hoped for a quiet few days. A chance to catch up on simple paperwork and certainly not having to brave the January cold.

DI Macleod and DS McGrath, the senior officers on his team, were at a conference that would change the way policing was achieved. At least, that was how the Inspector had worded it. It was a forced effort by him, of course, because it meant policies to do with how they spoke to each other. Every modernisation, especially in terms of how officers addressed each other or dressed, was painfully endured by the Inspector with a face held tight in a grimace. Ross believed if Macleod had not been so good at detecting crimes then he would have been pensioned off long ago.

Ross waved away a cup of tea placed in front of him and then watched the deckhand calmly take a slug of the liquid,

1

quickly as the boat rose. The cup was secured at the man's side as the boat fell back down off the wave. Ross no doubt would have covered himself in tea.

His destination on this blowy January day was Morning Light, a fledgling community built on the Monach Islands, just west of Benbecula. Over the last year a small community of idealists, according to his internet, had built a paradise, somewhere free from the soot and smog of everyday life—an eco-haven. Ross had nothing against such developments, but it seemed that the new heaven was now somewhat tainted. This morning, a woman had been discovered dead in the town square. And with his bosses away, Ross, as the more senior officer, had been dispatched to check on the death.

It was not common for a senior officer to attend a 'normal' death, but this one had become more complicated in that the woman's wrists were slit in an apparent act of suicide. The attending Sergeant who had arrived in the morning to the islands had thought that the scene was somewhat inconsistent with a suicide, mentioning that the blood at the scene seemed very meagre. The photographs he had sent through made Ross's police senses prick up too and after a quick word with the Inspector, he had got into his car and headed for the airport with a member of the forensic team.

Lucy MacTaggart was barely thirty and was a rather closed individual. Her comments, while not unkind in content, always seemed to be delivered with a dispassion, or a complete unawareness of their effect. But Jona Nakamura, her boss, had said she was as thorough as they came.

Lucy was sitting at the aft of the boat, watching the sea and Ross hated her for the simple ease she had while he looked like a clown, holding his stomach tightly. He tried to focus on what was ahead and soon saw the newly built harbour. It was more like a long pier bent around in a curve, presumably to provide shelter from the rough seas, and Ross longed for the vessel to come alongside.

Once they had docked, Ross stepped off the vessel to be greeted by Constable Allen who led him along a paved road to what looked like a small but modern village. Ross was taken aback by the quaintness of the place, stuck as it was on an island off Scotland's west coast, not somewhere which looked idyllic in January. Instead, it should seem harsh and barren but with newly fallen snow, the town of wooden buildings before him certainly could earn a place in any tourist guidebook.

That was until he saw the black coverall lying on the floor, surrounded by some other black coverings. The morbid tableau was up against a statue of a lighthouse which had a glowing light at its peak. The statue was surrounded by five houses built from logs, but with what seemed like modern windows and small units attached to the sides, possibly air source heat pumps or some other sort of heating system. The town square was empty except for another police officer, this time with the rank of Sergeant.

'Sergeant Tom Sutherland, and you must be DC Ross. Thanks for coming over. I guess you should call me Tom, what with this conference that's going on. What should I call you?'

'Ross is fine, Tom. I'm always Ross. Where is everyone? I'd have thought they would be gawking over the body like in most places.'

The Sergeant shook his head. 'Been ordered back to their homes by the mayor so as not to contaminate the scene.'

'Ordered?'

'Yes, that was how Mayor Forester put it. They have quite a tight community out here from what I've heard. When the idea of making an idyllic community was first floated, there was a lot of derision. I believe the mayor sees this place as a standard for all new builds to come, in terms of energy efficiency and also of community. But I'll let him bore you with all that. He's more than willing to tell anyone that will listen.'

Ross pulled his jacket around him and was thankful he had worn his hiking boots to this job. Snow was lying three inches thick and there was a dusting on top of the black coveralls.

'Shall we take a look, Ross?' asked a voice beside him. Turning, he saw Lucy MacTaggart already dressed in a white coverall and sporting gloves and a facemask.

'Please, be my guest. I'll stand at a distance so as not to contaminate anything.'

'I doubt you'll contaminate it any more than it already is. If we don't get to these kinds of instances fast, then the local population always make a hash of the scene.'

Ross stepped back and watched Lucy draw back the coverings. On the ground beside the statue, he saw brown hair leading down to a woman dressed in a flimsy but large t-shirt, sporting a comic mouse on the front. Bare white legs stuck out beyond her and a red stain was on the snow. Ross watched Lucy trace her hands around the body without disturbing anything and then give a grunt.

'I'm going to photograph her first,' she said to Ross, 'and then I'll check her over. Sergeant?'

'Yes,' said the officer, 'Sergeant Tom Sutherland. Or Tom as it is now.'

Lucy seemed to stare right through the man as if he had stated the most obvious thing in the world. 'Hold the covers,

4

Tom. There's not much of a wind but we need to be careful. And don't get in the way of the photographs.'

The Sergeant glanced over at Ross who simply shook his shoulders. Looking around him, Ross could see people at the windows of the houses. There were two younger women in one, one of whom seemed teary eyed. In another, an older couple looked on. A third had a man and woman of around thirty holding each other tight as they looked. A fourth was a smaller house and dark inside while the last house had an older man watching the other houses. This struck Ross as the other spectators were watching the square—not each other.

'Tell me, Tom, are there any buildings other than these?'

'Yes, there're two more homes. We're on Ceann Ear but there're two more islands that are interlinked at low tide. There's a family on Shivinish and a couple on Ceann Iar. I haven't seen anyone from there yet, but the mayor said that he had messaged them not to come over until the situation was dealt with.'

'And the woman before us is Amanda Novak?'

The Sergeant nodded. 'At least the mayor says so. He said she was Canadian, but we have not had any positive ID from any relative. Though having so few people here it's unlikely to be anyone else. They would know their own.'

'Is that her house?' asked Ross, pointing to the one house that was dark inside.'

'Yes, but we haven't gone inside. I've asked everyone to stay clear of it as well. Thought it best to get forensics here first. I wasn't convinced with the body, Ross. Too little blood for a suicide. I doubt it would have washed away.'

'It's a good thought,' mused Ross, but he was desperate for Lucy to begin an examination of the body and put that blessed camera down. The snow began again before Lucy set her camera aside and carefully started to run her hands across the unfortunate woman's body. At first, Lucy seemed almost uninterested as she examined the corpse but then she began to lift up the long t-shirt at the rear.

'Ross, over here,' shouted Lucy above a freshening wind.

Ross stepped carefully around the scene and knelt beside Lucy who was holding the t-shirt up at the back presenting a view of the woman's bare buttocks and back. 'What am I looking at?'

'That!' said Lucy, pointing at what looked like a minor disturbance of the flesh.'

'And?'

'It's a puncture wound.' Lucy pushed her finger into the small cut and it opened up. Ross watched in amazement as her finger disappeared inside. 'My guess is it's longer than that, right into the innards. Given the angle, I'd say the heart was potentially stabbed through.'

'But what about her wrists?'

'Probably cut after. But I doubt she was wearing this t-shirt when it all happened. There's no puncture hole in the top and the Sergeant was correct in that there seems to be too little blood around. Hardly any on the top. Something's wrong here. My money is on our girl being murdered somewhere else and then brought here, like a staged suicide.'

Ross, sitting on his haunches, thought through what this meant. He was on a remote island and Lucy was telling him there was a killer amongst this small group of people. Staring up, Ross glanced around the houses looking in on him, and the faces staring back.

'How long has she been dead?'

'Hard to be specific but I reckon it was in the night so dead anytime from nine until three this morning.'

As Ross pondered this, a door opened and a stout man with greying hair marched across the snow. He was wrapped up in a florescent jacket and wore wellington boots. Watching the Sergeant step across to block the man's path, Ross stood up and joined the barricade.

'Can we bury her? We can't have her lying there in front of everyone while you prod around Amanda's body. It's not right.'

'Mayor, please return to your house until my colleagues have completed their investigations.' The Sergeant was doing his best, but the Mayor was trying to force his way past.

'Excuse me, sir, my name is DC Ross and I'm currently running this investigation. May I ask that you return to your house and await us? I'm going to need to interview everyone.'

'But cover her up, man. She's right in the view of everyone.'

'Then I suggest that you close your curtains, Mayor . . . I apologise, sir, what is your name?'

The man was taken aback as Ross seemed focused on a matter of routine politeness. 'Mayor Forester.'

'And I believe you have some degree of responsibility over this town.'

'Yes, I'm the Mayor of Morning Light. We're a peaceful place, a better place. But we can't allow your colleague to brandish Amanda's body about like that—'

'Then get me a tent.'

Ross had been told about Lucy's occasional tacit response to being questioned about what she was doing. For a man of infinite patience and smooth running, Ross was taken aback by the casual barb, but he was not going to have a scene develop.

Placing a hand behind the man and showing the way back to the Mayor's house with the other, Ross began to walk him to this front door.

'Normally, we would have a tent but as you can imagine getting hold of something such as that out here is not easy. But if you can remain inside and maybe close your curtains, then I'll be with you shortly to take statements.'

'But the girl killed herself. It would be the decent thing to bury her. Right here where she loved. She was one of us, officer.'

'Indeed, but it appears something was amiss, so I need to take the appropriate measures.' Ross gave a firm but compassionate grin.

'But with the storm coming, we need to hurry to place her in the ground or we'll not be able to for a few days.'

'Inside, Mayor. I'll be along shortly. Thank you for your cooperation.'

Storm, thought Ross, *great*. He pulled his mobile from his pocket and dialled Inspector Macleod.

'Ross, thank goodness, do you need me?'

'I'm afraid so. We have a dead woman on our hands and Lucy MacTaggart believes she was murdered, not suicide as originally thought. I think this is as remote as I've been, sir. I could do with some help.'

'Okay, you know the drill, site secured and then get some initial statements. I'll get Hope to get some more officers your way if we can.'

'Hope, sir?' Ross asked, taken aback.

'Yes, Hope, your boss, Ross. Or do you want Alan? That'll take some getting used to.'

'Sir?'

'Never mind, I'll tell you when I see you. Ring Jona, too.'

Ross stared at his mobile for a moment, somewhat confused. But then he walked over to the Sergeant. 'Weather going to get bad?'

The man nodded. 'I'm not sure if the boat will be able to come back later tonight, Ross. It looks like it'll be us for the moment, at least until morning but even then, I'm not hopeful.'

'Okay, Sergeant, but be aware that your initial suspicions were correct, Tom. This woman was murdered, and the killer's probably watching us through one of the windows. We need to play this one very carefully.'

Ross stepped away and watched Lucy working on the body at the foot of the statue. He would have a lot of work to do before his boss got here and he'd need to keep everyone safe. Suddenly, the weather seemed even colder.

Chapter 2

Ross consulted the Sergeant and left Lucy MacTaggart to her work while he and the senior uniformed officer made their way to speak to the mayor of Morning Light. Constable Allen was detailed to assist Lucy as necessary but Ross doubted she would seek much help.

Mayor Duncan Forester was opening his front door as Ross and Sergeant Tom Sutherland approached and the man quickly hailed them inside, indicating that the weather was too rough to be standing outside.

'Mayor Forester, that's better to be inside; it's a rough day for sure,' said Ross.

'Please Officer, let me take your coat and come inside. My daughter Autumn has the kettle on so maybe I could offer you some tea?' Mayor Forester was a tall and thick-set man who Ross could see in the second row of a rugby scrum. His hands looked more like shovels and his thick black hair was neatly combed into place. Adorned in a woollen jumper, the man led the pair of officers through to a living room that had a wood-fuelled stove. The mayor noticed Ross staring at the flames.

'Ah yes, it is a little conceit of mine. Generally, all our heat and electricity are taken care of by the wind turbines and wave power devices we have around the island, but we do allow ourselves the luxury of a real fire when it's really cold. Of course, we have to ship that wood in as we don't have any actual woods to speak of here. We had given thought to it but that would limit the numbers we could grow to.'

'Of course,' said Ross, not fully attentive but instead taking a moment to place his hands in front of the stove to receive some warmth. 'I'm going to need to interview the residents, Mayor. I'm quite happy to do that in their own homes and that might be easiest as it will keep anyone from speaking to anyone else.'

'Would that be a problem?' The mayor took up a seat in a large wooden rocking chair on the far side of the room.

'It's just a matter of routine, sir. Prevents anyone from absently repeating what anyone else has told them rather than what they actually know.'

'But, of course. I should have thought of that. Ah, here's Autumn.'

Ross took his hands from in front of the fire and turned to see a red-headed teenager holding a tray featuring four mugs, a sugar bowl, and a number of spoons. The girl looked up at Ross from under her straggly hair and he thought he saw a smile. Gingerly, she presented the tray in front of him and he stared at the cups before him.

'It's Rooibos tea, Officer. We try not to have anything too harmful to ourselves like coffee or tea but there is a small supply if you need some,' advised the mayor.

'It's fine,' said Ross, and then remembered his colleague. 'That okay for yourself, Sergeant Sutherland?'

The officer nodded and Ross took a mug of the steaming

infusion. The girl waited, large green eyes staring at him until he realised she was waiting to see if he would take sugar. Ross waved her away gently and noticed she was still staring at him, even as she offered the tray to Sergeant Sutherland.

'It's such a tragic thing to happen,' began the Mayor, 'but Amanda was a little strange, Officer.'

'How so?'

'Well, for one, she was a loner. Everyone else on these islands lives with someone. We're a rather diverse community, intentionally so. We have Orla and Kiera, partners, living here, Alfie and Edna, an old married couple, and Daniella and Paul, unmarried but what society would call a normal couple. On the other islands are the Arnold family, six of them, parents and children ranging from twenty to six. And then there's Celeste and Hamish—she's much older than him.'

'Quite an array of different types of families,' offered Tom Sutherland.

'Quite, and deliberately made so. You see here in Morning Light, we are trying to be different, and Amanda was chosen for that reason. Whilst it has been great to have families move here, we did want to have at least one person who was of the single lifestyle.'

'Hold up,' said Ross. 'Before you tell me more, could you fill me in with some details about this place? I'm not sure I heard much about it which seems strange given the kind of commune and ideals you have suggested. How long have you been going?'

Mayor Forester got to his feet and walked over to a picture on the wall. 'That was all of us eighteen months ago, moving into our homes. We kept it extremely low key, Constable, as we are not here for public entertainment. All of us genuinely want a better life in cleaner air and with supportive people around us.' The man stopped speaking and began to look at the floor. Ross held his peace and saw the man begin to sniff. 'I'm sorry, Officer, but I don't know why Amanda did that to herself. It's not what any one of us would have wanted.'

Ross saw the man's daughter walk to her father and place an arm around him causing the man to turn and hold his child.

'I'm sure it's difficult for everyone, sir,' said Ross, 'but tell me, you said Amanda liked the single lifestyle but was she friendly enough in the community?'

'Mandy kept herself to herself generally, not that she was in any way rude. She would talk to you if you spoke to her, but she said extraordinarily little about herself. She took her turn in the various activities we have here, but she was rather silent if things got onto a personal level in any conversation.'

'And she had been here eighteen months?'

'Oh, no. Mandy had been with us six months. We started off with Ken Arnold, Uncle of the Arnold children on the other island but he left after six months as the solitude didn't really work out for him. Personally, I think he needed company, personal company if you understand me, and we don't have any free spirits here, just attached partners. While we try to embrace anyone's lifestyle, there are no open relationships on the islands as far as I know.'

'And certainly none Ken could take advantage of, if he left,' stated the Sergeant.

'Indeed. After Ken we had Susan, Susan Godwin. A lovely girl, really bright and outgoing but she moved on, too. Haven't heard from her since which was a shock as she left on good terms.'

Ross sipped on his infusion and thought for a moment.

There was a lot of information coming at him at once and he could do with taking it down. Macleod seemed to hold everything from a conversation in his head, but Ross was not like the boss.

Part of Ross wanted to tell the mayor that his quiet resident had not killed herself but had been murdered but that was better kept quiet until he knew what the residents on the islands knew.

'I need to talk in a bit more detail about the last twenty-four hours, Mayor Forester, specifically about Amanda's movements and your own. It's all purely routine to help us build a picture. Can you tell me who found her outside in the town square?'

'That was Autumn, my daughter. She came into my bedroom this morning and indicated there was something unusual outside. It was still dark, but I put on my jacket and boots and found Amanda lying there. I checked her over and found her wrists slit and no pulse. I got hold of Alfie Collins as he has some medical training and he confirmed she was dead. I didn't want to move her, so we called the police and then the Sergeant and his colleague came over. I've been keeping everyone back as I didn't want anything to disturb the scene.'

'So, the only people to have actually touched Amanda since you found her have been yourself and Mr Collins—that correct?' asked Ross, his notebook now out and his pencil feverishly writing away.

'That's correct.'

'Miss Forester, is it correct you woke your father this morning on seeing something unusual outside?' The red-haired girl nodded and smiled whilst keeping her eyes on Ross. 'And what time was that?' The girl continued to smile and then

14

held up five fingers.

'She means five o'clock.'

'No need to be shy,' said Ross, 'it's all extremely helpful. Can you tell me what was unusual about what you saw?' The girl said nothing and Ross raised his eyebrows. 'It's okay, you can tell me; I'm a police officer.'

The girl gave a broad smile and then began to move her fingers at speed in what Ross believed to be sign language. Giving a slight smile as well, he signed back his thanks. It had been six months since the course and he doubted he would ever use sign language in anger, but he had kept it going and was finding that although he was scrabbling to keep up, he could understand most of what the girl was saying.

'What age are you?' Ross signed as he spoke.

Eighteen came the silent reply.

'Mr Forester, as your daughter is technically an adult, I would like to interview her alone. It's standard procedure for an adult.'

'Is that really necessary?'

It was not but Ross wanted to have the girl's independent opinion on what had happened. He was worried that her father would fill in the blanks for her and as he had a murdered victim outside, Ross was making sure he trusted no one at this time.

'It's just standard procedure, sir, that's all. I'll be interviewing all of you on your own, so I need to treat your daughter with the same respect. That's not an issue, is it?'

The man shook his head, but his face said otherwise. 'Okay, Autumn, can you wait outside, please. I'll be with you in a minute.' Ross signed and spoke as he had been taught when doing his training. With those who did not sign in the room it was at least a courtesy.

'What more can you tell me about Amanda Novak, Mayor Forester?' asked Ross when Autumn had left the room.

'Not a lot. Like I said she was a loner even though she lived right here. Said little.'

'When did you last see her before Autumn alerted you to her presence outside this morning?'

The man sat back in his chair and thought. 'It was yesterday afternoon. She had taken herself for a walk and was returning. Amanda seemed happy enough. She exchanged a few words with Autumn.'

'She could sign?'

'Yes, not like me. My wife did that. Unfortunately, June passed away three years ago.'

Ross watched the man's face for a flicker of sadness or regret, but none came. 'I imagine that was rough on Autumn.'

'It was indeed. But in truth she's better off without her mother. One of the reasons I'm here is that June had become a junkie and that's what killed her. Started with alcohol and then turned into drugs. That's why we needed a clean start and here was perfect.'

'Regarding that, how did this whole community start up? I mean, I see what are quite elaborate houses, given where we are. You have your own power supply. I assume you grow vegetables and other things, or do you just take in supplies. What I'm saying is I imagine none of this comes cheap, and there must be someone behind this.'

Mayor Forester nodded and stood up again from his rocking chair, walking once again over to the wall and to a rather large photograph. Ross saw the mayor in the picture along with an older gentleman. 'That's Viscount Donoghue, the proud sponsor of our lifestyle. We all paid in as well, but the main capital costs were by his company. He's a sixties' child, I guess you would say. A bit too much free love and earth mother for my liking but he has similar beliefs to me in how to live. And anyway, Autumn needed this place.'

I'll need to get Stewart onto the background of this place, thought Ross, and that made him think about something else.

'You have telephone signal here. Do you have Wi-Fi too?'

'Oh yes, we're not technophobes here; indeed, it's essential to the schooling of the children amongst us, and to many of us who work for a living. The mobile works through the Wi-Fi; it's a little transceiver we have that routes the calls through the net to the mainland where the connection with the phone network is made. There's a subsea cable from the island. That's where the real money was spent as that cost a packet. But it is essential in these days. I think we marry technology and sustainable living together.'

'Okay, Mayor, I may need more but basically you saw a reasonably happy Amanda yesterday after coming back from a walk and that was that until this morning.' The man nodded. 'Okay, I'll speak to your daughter next and then I'll go one-by-one around the other houses. We'll also need to take a look in Amanda's home.'

'That shouldn't be a problem. We don't lock our doors here.' The man coughed. 'I don't want to sound indelicate but when can we bury her? She's one of us and she should return to the island soil.'

'Well, I need to get hold of her family. Do you have any contacts?'

The man shook his head again. 'She was very private, like I say.'

'Once we do that, we'll need to do an autopsy. The body will

17

need to go to the mainland. After that, where she is buried will depend on the family or any express wishes left behind by her, or so I would imagine. Once it's released from the investigation then it's beyond my jurisdiction.'

Mayor Forester stood up and his face had a degree of anger to it. The teeth were clenched and Ross saw the man's fist curl. 'Autopsy? Why the hell would we need an autopsy? Look at the weather, man. She needs to be buried. She killed herself, plain and simple. We don't need this to go rumbling on and some outside copper looking for promotion try to make a big deal of nothing.'

Ross cocked his head to one side to let the man know he was being assessed. It was not a habit of Ross's but he had learnt that a little misdirection often broke the concentration or anger of a person. 'It's interesting that you seem so quick to move Miss Novak onto the next world, Mayor. I wasn't going to say but I feel the need to inform you officially as the closest thing to a town representative here. We are treating Miss Novak's death as suspicious, so your full co-operation is requested.'

'As you wish.'

If the man had raged, Ross would have seen it as normal. If the man had sank to his knees in shock, Ross would not have been surprised. But the comment made Ross nervous. Was the man simply keen to protect the island's reputation, or was he up to his neck in this?

Chapter 3

R oss stepped out of the house into the town square and felt an icy blast on his cheek. His conversation with Autumn had revealed little. The sky was dark, the light was fading fast, and behind him, he heard Sergeant Sutherland clap his hands together.

'Snow is on the way, Ross; how do you want to play it from here?'

Ross nodded and looked around the square. The first thought in his mind was that Lucy McTaggart would want the body to be moved once she had completed her necessary first investigations. Ideally that would be a place that would house the team as well. With the prospect of no back-up being able to get here, or indeed arrive in a hurry if anything else was amiss, Ross wanted to keep the evidence close and his team tight so as to guarantee their safety.

The second thought was that he should get all names and details off to Kirsten Stewart back at their Inverness office and let her loose on compiling as much background detail on the islanders as possible. Macleod would also need to be informed. After that he would interview the rest of the small population, including the people on the other islands.

Approaching Lucy McTaggart, who was still hunched over the body of Amanda Novak, he coughed gently before realising she could not hear him above the rising wind. Ross tapped her shoulder, and the forensic officer waved her hand at him without looking. Stepping back, Ross waited a moment for Lucy to finish whatever she was up to. Looking around, he saw the folk of the island staring at him from their windows, including the mayor.

'Yes,' said Lucy, turning around suddenly.

'Was wondering if you wanted the body moved before the weather really sets in? Looks like a blizzard on the way and I think the winds are due to rocket.'

'Of course,' said Lucy dismissively.

Ross stepped closer to speak into her ear and she drew back until he grabbed her shoulder pulling her close. 'Lucy, I think we should keep all evidence close to us as I reckon we have a killer in this community. So, for safety, and protection of evidence, I am going to ask for somewhere to stay which can accommodate the body.' As he stepped back, Lucy seemed nonchalant, as if it were no news to her.

'I'll be ready to move her in about ten minutes. That should beat your storm.'

Ross nodded and gave a smile which received an emotionless expression in return. Calling Sergeant Sutherland to him, he asked the man to contact Kirsten Stewart in the Inverness office and to furnish her with all the names of the islanders and to ask her to conduct a thorough search into who they were. She was also to advise Inspector Macleod of what was happening and to let him know Ross, himself, would check in later.

Having made his requests, Ross returned to the mayor's

house and was forced to rap the door, something he found strange, for he knew the mayor had been watching.

'Mayor Forester, we're going to need to prepare for the night. Looking at the storm coming, we need to get the body of Amanda Novak somewhere safe and my team could do with some shelter as well. Where is there that we can use?'

The man furrowed his face but then seemed to have a revelation. 'The community hall would be ideal for you, Officer. It has toilets, hot and cold water, and I'm sure we can get some mattresses and blankets in there for you, although we do have heating.'

Ross nodded but looked around him. 'Sorry to ask but what sort of heating. I haven't seen any oil tanks or any smoking chimneys. I know you have a stove but that wouldn't be running a hall.'

The mayor chortled and then became more serious. 'We have geothermal power, heat from below the ground. You'll be warm enough, Officer Ross. Do you all want to sleep over there, or shall we find some other digs for your female colleague? They all seem to be getting younger these days.'

Ross had in no way appreciated Lucy for her looks but now he thought about, maybe certain men and women might see her in that light. As for Ross, he just saw someone who had been described to him as brilliant but on the spectrum, and who appeared to be cold to any warming advances of friendship, or simple colleague camaraderie.

It was ten minutes later, after Lucy's say so, that Ross, Sergeant Tom Sutherland, and Constable Allen carried the body of Amanda Novak over to a community hall that lay outside the main gathering of houses. As the mayor had said, it was warm, contained a main hall, and had an extra room

21

tagged onto the rear.

Ross divided the main hall into a work area at the front and a small impromptu mortuary at the rear, screening it with some large dividers found in the hall's storage cupboards. The mayor and his daughter led the constable to and fro with mattresses and blankets, but Ross noted none of the other residents seemed to be helping. Indeed, none came out of their houses. It was now six o'clock and while his temporary office was functional, Ross realised he needed some sustenance. Again, the mayor arrived with cans of soup and Constable Allen made up the basic rations, delivering it to Ross with some large chunks of bread. As he was enjoying them, Sergeant Sutherland approached.

'What is it, Tom? You seem very bothered.'

'Boat's not running, Ross. They said the water's whipped up and it's not safe. Helos won't fly either what with the wind that's about to hit us.' As if on cue, Ross heard a bout of hail hit the windows of the hall.

'Well, then, we had better get comfortable. I want to interview the rest of the islanders tonight but rather than get them here, let's go see them in their houses. Take the constable and tell them to expect us, please, Sergeant. After that, Allen can stay here with Lucy and we'll do the interviews. Also, let's make sure we can lock this place up. I'm thinking of standing guard over our body tonight.'

'You are? All night?'

'Not just me, in turns, Sergeant. Something's making me uneasy.'

Tom Sutherland gave a quiet nod and cocked an ear to the wind. 'I'm not sure we'll get much sleep 'til morning anyhow.'

When their meal was finished, Ross took a briefing from

Lucy. The wound to the body was very subtle and Lucy wondered if it would have been spotted by a cursory glance. The cut wrists were obvious but the puncture on the rear of the body had been made by something smooth and narrow and delivered with constant force. The skin had closed back over but Lucy had been giving the body a thorough going over.

'So, it's like someone wanted us to think suicide and was banking on no autopsy. Is that normal not to have one when suicide is committed?'

'It's up to the Procurator Fiscal but if there's little doubt, why bother with an autopsy. The Sergeant did well in recognising the issue of a lack of blood. We should be searching the island to see if we can find the missing blood; see if it's smeared on anywhere or has contaminated clothing.'

'Let's bear that in mind, Lucy but I don't want to force a situation here, where someone feels they have to strike out again. I'll interview tonight and you can take a look at Amanda Novak's house with Constable Allen, see if you can find anything. But don't separate.'

Lucy gave Ross a look of sheer contempt, like he had told her she was stupid, and walked off. Rising from his seat, he asked Sergeant Sutherland if he had obtained a means for locking the building.

'Yes, Ross, I have all the keys, or at least those the mayor has owned up to. It'll have to do.'

The hall was a mere hundred yards from the houses, but the snow was now blowing a blizzard and Ross held his hand up to his face to prevent the cavalcade of white from covering his eyes. With his small team, he walked into the town square and watched Lucy and Allen make their way to Amanda Novak's house while Sutherland and himself rapped on the door of a young couple.

Ross had seen one of the women at the window and had been rather shocked that she was wearing a dressing gown, which only made it to her knees and a pair of rainbow socks that almost touched the knee. By contrast the door was opened by a dour young woman dressed in a large white jumper and wearing a thick charcoal skirt with a pair of dark slippers beneath.

'Good evening ma'am, I'm DC Ross and behind me is Sergeant Fletcher. We need to ask you a few questions about the sad demise of your neighbour.'

'Very well.' The stolid woman before him stood absolutely still and Ross wondered if he was meant to ask these questions in the middle of the blizzard. But his fears were unfounded as a voice called from the other room.

'Orla, let them in or they'll freeze to death. Nothing to hide in here.' The stolid woman briefly stepped back, and Ross rushed past and into the warm living room the other voice had shouted from. The girl in the dressing gown was now lounging in front of the heartily burning stove and her gown was open revealing a t-shirt and briefs which made Ross start despite his own sexuality.

'Kiera, for God's sake, cover yourself,' shouted the stolid woman. Kiera flung her dressing gown over her body but gave a cheeky smile to the officers.

'Sorry to bother you but as you know, your neighbour, Amanda Novak, is dead and I need to ask you a few questions about her and her death. Can I get your names first, for the record?'

'Orla, Orla McIlroy,' said the stolid girl, her Northern Irish accent now becoming clear without the wind to disturb the sound. 'And this is Kiera Harris, my partner.'

Inside, some part of Ross rebelled against this idea, as the women were so different. But you could never tell in relationships. 'And how long have you been together?'

'Two years,' said Orla, 'got together not long before we came here. It seemed an ideal place to live, away from all those snide remarks you get. You have no idea how cruel the world can be.'

Actually, thought Ross, *I really do.*

'But it has gone to Kiera's head being here. As you can see, she's not very prim and proper as a woman should be.'

With that Kiera opened her gown and laughed before closing it again. 'Lighten up, Orls; it's not like I'm nude underneath.'

'Hardly appropriate though with someone deceased and being interviewed,' said Sergeant Sutherland. 'Were you not fond of Amanda Novak? I mean in a small place like this I reckon you'd have to get along.'

'I was actually,' laughed Kiera, 'very fond. She lightened up the more she was here too. When she first arrived, she was morbid but then she picked up. Remember that time she was drunk and we—'

'Kiera! No need to speak ill of the dead.'

'It's fine, Miss McIlroy,' said Ross, 'what happened, Kiera?'

'She tried to get it on with Orla, right out there in the square. Of course, Orla had no part of it but I came to Amanda's rescue. Orla just watching noting something in her notebook. I think she was keeping tabs. Were you, Orla?'

'I just had my diary in my hand, that's all. But you were shameful.'

'And she likes a bit of shameful,' laughed Kiera.

'Can we just calm down a moment?' pleaded Ross. 'So,

25

Amanda Novak changed while she was here.'

'She was quiet when she arrived,' said a prim Miss McIlroy, 'but as she got to know people, she loosened up quite considerably, too much I would say. And there was obviously a sadness behind her. You can see that now, we all can.'

'So, you reckon she killed herself because she was sad?' asked Ross. 'You don't think someone might have done it to her?'

'Good grief, Officer, what makes you say such a thing?' Orla was outraged but Kiera stood up now and dropped her gown, standing in a what she may have thought as a provocative pose. 'Well, I wouldn't have killed her, I was sleeping with her.'

'You slept with her once,' cried Orla, 'and that was enough.'

'As far as you knew.'

Ross spied a bottle on the seat Kiera had been sitting on. Glancing at the Sergeant, he then motioned to Orla to take a hold of her partner. Ross watched closely as the woman stood up and then almost gingerly placed a hand on Kiera's shoulder and then one underneath her opposite armpit.

'We'll get a glass of water, but frankly, Officer, all we know is that when we woke up this morning the poor woman was out there having slit her wrists. We didn't see her yesterday and last night, we went to bed at eight. So, I'm afraid there's nothing more to tell except she was a rather lonely figure, keeping herself to herself. Now excuse me while I get Kiera a drink of water. Come on, walk!'

There was nothing personal in Orla's touch to Kiera. Nothing that indicated any sort of love to Ross. He suspected there was more to this relationship than what he was hearing, and maybe a touch of jealousy so he was not going to leave the story as it was. But he would need Kiera on her own, and that was not going to happen at the moment; the girl was too drunk.

'Not the most useful,' said Sergeant Sutherland as the pair let themselves out of the house. Making their way next door, Ross saw his feet crunch through the newly delivered snow but could not hear them for the howl of the wind. Standing before the next house, he knocked loudly but no one answered. Again, he banged on the door before moving to the large window that showed a living room with two elderly people sitting in armchairs before a fire.

The eyes were open, so they were not asleep. Ross banged loudly on the window and the woman turned briefly in her chair squinting at him. Then she turned back to her fire and closed her eyes. Ross shook his head. *Where did they get these people from?*

Chapter 4

'You could try the door, Ross; the mayor said they don't lock them here,' said Sergeant Sutherland.

'I'm not standing out here,' Ross yelled over the storm, hoping the occupants of the house could hear him. Reaching forward, he grabbed a door handle and found it moved easily. Opening and holding the door for his colleague, Ross caught an icy blast of wind on his face and hurried inside. Stamping his feet, which were now covered in snow, he unzipped his jacket and called out for the owners. When no reply came, he shook his head at Sutherland and simply opened the door off the hallway to the living room.

'Excuse me, sir, ma'am, Detective Constable Ross and my colleague is Sergeant Sutherland. Would it be possible to have a word with you? I did knock but you did not seem to be responding.'

The woman turned round in her seat which had its back to Ross. She then turned back and tapped the man's arm.

'What, woman?' came the man's cry.

'People here, Alfie. I think they're police. It might be to do with Amanda.'

'Do you really think so? Bloody genius, you!' The man forced himself from his chair and turned to face Ross. 'What do you want, and who are you?'

'I did say, sir, DC Ross, and I am here in connection with the death of Amanda Novak.'

The man shook his head violently. 'Get on with it then. Coming out in this weather—really, you should be ashamed. We were just relaxing and you bring up this dark subject with my wife.'

Ross was taken aback but showed little of it and instead pulled his notebook out in a calm manner. 'If I could first ask for your names.'

'Did the Mayor not give you our names? You could have asked him?'

'Sir, calm down and please, sit down, I'll come round so you can stay in front of your stove.' Now that he was inside, Ross was beginning to feel the heat from the stove and unzipped his jacket fully.

'Just be quick about it, officer, I don't want my wife upset.'

'Okay sir. Now can I ask you for your names, please?'

'Alfred and Edna Collins.'

'And how long have you been on the island?'

'Since we all came across. Peaceful, you see. Well, until Madam went and did that to herself. I said to Edna, you watch, they'll all be over now. Sure, it will start with your sort but pretty soon the papers will be here, looking for photos and giving out some nonsense about this place.'

Ross held up a hand and the man stopped. 'Can you just answer the question, sir? I'll do my best to be out of your hair as quick as I can, but I need to know some details. Now, how well did you get on with Amanda Novak?'

The man sat down and held his wife's hand. 'She was a bit off. We try to accept all people, but she was awfully close to herself, if you understand me. Not very pleasant, cut you dead as soon as look at you. In truth, we kept our distance. It's a shame but she was not contributing to this society, keeping herself to herself. She'll not be missed.'

'Sounds very harsh, sir. Mrs Collins, do you agree with your husband's assessment of your neighbour?'

Edna Collins looked at her husband and then at Ross. Her grey hair was held tight to her head by a scrunchy at the rear of her head and her face looked just as strained. Several times she glanced from one man to the other before beginning to sob.

'My wife is not very well these days, officer; she gets easily upset. But we live life together so I doubt there's any more she could add for you.'

Ross nodded, seeing the woman's tears continue. 'Where were you both over this last forty-eight hours and did you see Amanda Novak during this time?'

'Life here, officer, is quite simple. We go to the biospheres to help look after the plants and that is what we were doing yesterday. We saw Amanda pass by them but otherwise, we did not see her all day. Like I said, she kept herself to herself. Although our doors are always open, we do not feel the need to run in and out of each other's homes like they do on those mainland estates. We chose this life to have some quiet. Most days we go from the crops to home. If the weather is good, we may take a stroll around some of the island. But in this weather, we stay home.'

'So, the first you knew something was amiss was when?'

'When the mayor woke us up. Took us by surprise. To be honest, I think it's still affecting Edna greatly.'

'Do you know anything further about Miss Novak?' asked

Ross.

'Only that she had asked for a cat at one point but at the moment we are allowed no animals. Just while we are getting everything set up. It takes a while to get used to a place and animals can be funny.'

Glancing at Sergeant Sutherland, Ross indicated to the man to speak if he thought there was anything further at this time. The man shook his shoulders and Ross thanked the couple before making his exit. As he zipped his jacket back up, an icy blast came through the open door.

'One more and then we check Miss Novak's house, Tom. I'm getting the feeling that this might be a waste of time interviewing everyone. They seem rather okay for having someone in such a community kill herself. Certainly not the most caring.'

Tom nodded and led the way to the last occupied house, knocking loudly on arrival. The door was answered by a middle-aged man in a tweed jacket, complimented by a smart pair of beige trousers. The man could only have been mid-thirties and Ross thought him dressed beyond his years.

'Hello, I guess you must be the police. We saw you earlier at Amanda's body. Incredibly sad.'

'That's right, sir. DC Ross and Sergeant Sutherland. We just need to ask you a few questions, preferably inside given the weather, sir.'

The man took the hint and stepped aside to allow the police officers access to his hallway. Ross noted the hall seemed full of ornate knick-knacks, or junk as his partner would have called them. The man ushered them into a similar-sized living room to the other houses they had been in but this one was in the shadow of a grandfather clock. It dominated the room and the man stood in admiration of it as he made sure his guests got an unobstructed view.

'Lovely, isn't she? Been with me the last ten years and in the dining hall at Bathview college before that for a hundred years. Just magnificent.'

'Indeed sir,' said Tom Sutherland, 'but could I ask for your name, please?'

'Oh, how silly, I'm Paul, Paul Kemp. I guess you need the full name, don't you? And my partner is in the kitchen, Daniella. Daniella White.' The man walked to the door and shouted, 'Daniella darling, come through, would you?'

Ross watched what he thought was the shape of a man but then quickly realised that the figure had a skirt and blouse on. Sergeant Sutherland was more taken aback, and Ross watched him struggle to maintain a straight face and not show some degree of shock. Despite his own lifestyle preferences, Ross struggled to not be jarred by the figure, but he smiled and said, 'This must be Daniella. How long have you been together?'

'Just over two years,' said Daniella, and took Paul by the arm. 'Little romancer, this one.'

'And you came out here,' said Ross. 'I guess it was to get away from comments and the like. Not right but maybe a wise move. I've had similar experiences.' Ross watched Tom Sutherland's face as he looked at Ross quizzically. A homosexual lifestyle was certainly seen to be more normal these days, but Ross found it still shocked some people despite the fact he never hid his true feelings.

'Well, yes,' said Daniella, 'easier as you say. Although some said we were traitors not standing up to things. But it's been great. The rest of our little group don't mind and well, it's such a lovely place if you like solitude.'

Ross nodded and took a seat offered by Paul, relaxing back into it. 'Can I get you a coffee, or tea, officer?'

'Absolutely,' said Ross, feeling more relaxed now than he had throughout his experience on the island. 'Coffee, black. And the Sergeant will have one too.' Ross had added that quickly because he saw Tom Sutherland was still struggling with Daniella's appearance. As Paul left for the kitchen, Ross sat forward and asked Daniella, 'How well did you know Amanda Novak?'

'Actually, she was a bit of a loner and she definitely avoided me. I tried to be civil, but some people just can't warm to my looks. I see your Sergeant is struggling.'

'Apologies,' said Tom Sutherland, 'my fault entirely. I don't mean to but, well, you certainly stand out.'

Ross saw Daniella laugh and then lean forward as if teasing the Sergeant. 'Back to Amanda, Miss White, if we can; did she seem in any way depressed to you?'

'Oh, Amanda was always up and down. One day she was smiling at Paul, always Paul mind, never me, and the next she was in a foul mood. And then she's as happy as Larry but vacant. Strange girl.'

'Had she tried anything like this before?' asked the sergeant, trying to refocus on his task.

'Not that I'm aware of but she was not here that long. There's been three tenants in that house, and they have all come and gone now. Maybe a solitary life doesn't suit people. I'm not sure. I wish I could tell you what was up with them all, but I think you need a partner to be here. Or an entire family, like the Arnolds.'

'That's the family on Shivinish, Ross,' advised Tom Sutherland.

33

'Lovely family,' continued Daniella, 'but they like their privacy at times. June Arnold is home schooling, so she likes not to be disturbed during the day, but we often see them over here during better weather if the tides allow. Hamish and Celeste are rather more standoffish. Bloody French for you, I guess.'

'Daniella, don't talk ill of our neighbours. Celeste is a lovely woman, just a little misunderstood.'

'She certainly catches Paul's eye. Still, she's two islands away so there's no harm.'

'I was asking Daniella if Amanda seemed in any way down,' said Ross.

'Well, she was all over the place, wasn't she, Dani? Nice enough girl to talk to but swings and roundabouts with her moods. Depends how you caught her. I guess she was just too darn lonely in the end.'

'Was she ever romantically engaged with anyone here?'

'No, not at all,' replied Paul. 'I can't even tell you about her life off the island. Kept herself to herself.'

Ross looked around the room and was amazed at the number of strange ornate items on the various shelves. He guessed in a way it was homely, but it reminded him of an antique shop. His mind was searching for something because Amanda had been murdered. As much as he did not want to give too much of his hand away, he was struggling to see any good reason why she should be killed.

Ross asked more questions, but every answer was the same about Amanda; no one knew anything about her. Contact Kirsten, that was the plan. She would dig up the dirt on all of them and then he might have something to go on. After he had drunk his coffee, Ross motioned to Sutherland that they were leaving, and they made their way back out into the snow.

'Don't you find it strange—' started Sutherland.

'Not here,' said Ross. 'They're watching us and maybe lipreading, who knows. But yes, Tom, I do.'

The pair trudged to the last house they had not been in. It was lit up now, a light in nearly every room and as he approached, he heard a cry from inside as the door opened.

'Tell them to put their bloody suits on, I don't want snow walked everywhere.'

The apologetic face of Constable Allen appeared. 'I'm sorry but Miss MacTaggart would like you both to wear suits inside the house.' By way of a demonstration, Allen indicated his own suit and then pointed to the plastic bag on the floor. 'She's quite insistent.'

'And so she should be,' said Ross. *More polite though, she should be more polite.* 'Where is Lucy, constable?'

Ross had not been asking for the officer's name, but he quickly volunteered, 'John. And she's upstairs in the woman's bedroom.'

'Excellent, John,' said Ross, taking the stairs to the upper floor and followed by the Sergeant. 'Lucy, tell me you have this case cracked because we have nothing but a lot of people who seemed to live in ignorance of this young woman.' Ross smiled as he spoke and he realised that for once he was out from under the reins of his superiors. He always thought of himself as a good-natured person, but he was having to be so diligent when the boss was around, and as for Hope, she was not always the most thorough on the minor matters.

'You need to give me longer to crack a case and anyhow, I thought that was your job. Mine is simply to furnish you with different pieces of forensic information, stunningly come by, of course.'

Ross searched Lucy's face for any sign of humour, but the woman was deadly serious. *On the spectrum they had said. They never say where on the spectrum, do they?*

'Have you found anything, Lucy?' asked Ross, this time refraining from his humorous overtones.

'The bed,' said the forensic officer, pointing to the uncovered mattress. 'It's full of sweat marks. She's either been going at full and frankly high-speed sex or she's been sweating in her sleep. Given the lack of semen I am suggesting the second.'

Again, Ross looked for the merest glimpse of a smile, something to say she had not thought this way of delivering the information was in any way normal—but there was no indication.

'Why was she sweating?'

'I need to get a look at what's in her system, Ross. I'm not a miracle worker. It would be better done in a mortuary. It's not exactly the best place to run tests. I haven't got much kit with me, more to do an initial analysis, not to break down every floated idea.'

'See what you can do. Anything else in the house?'

'Not that I can find. Her prints on the mirror but I haven't found anything untoward. I sent John off for a look because he whistles, which is bloody annoying and something you would have thought he would have been taught not to do.'

Ross shook his head and stepped outside the room to find John on the landing. 'Lucy says she sent you round the house. Find anything?'

'Nothing unusual, Ross. Food in the cupboards, fuel for the stove. There's a computer but the history only has shopping sites, BBC, ITV, and other TV channels. Think she might have watched Netflix on there too and a few other bits and pieces.'

'So, nothing showing stress or that?'

'No, sir.'

Ross decided that he would need to complete a full walk-through of the house himself to be entirely satisfied and began upstairs. The house was not particularly large and besides the bedroom there was only a box room and a bathroom. Ross thought there were very few cosmetic products for a woman, although that may have been her choice.

On the ground floor, he found a quaint sitting room, almost like a hut from a retreat brochure. The kitchen was stocked with the basic essentials, a set of pans that were in stainless steel. The cutlery was simple, possibly from an unremarkable set. There was a standard salt cellar and a range of glasses he recognised from a Swedish superstore.

At the rear of the kitchen was a tiny room with washer and dryer. A pair of green wellies sat neatly at the rear door. Going back upstairs, Ross checked the wardrobe and found a selection of clothing, neatly hanging or folded into the drawers.

Returning downstairs, Ross stood at the window and looked out into the town square. The scene was dimly lit by the lights on the outside of the houses, solar-powered batteries keeping them illuminated if Ross was not mistaken.

'I can't see anything strange, Ross,' said Sutherland, interrupting Ross's thoughts. 'Everything looks normal.'

'Indeed,' mused Ross. 'Not a single strange t-shirt, or weird piece of underwear. Something silly from a holiday, that awful keepsake a friend gave, some small bit of crap from a Christmas cracker. Nothing, absolutely nothing. This could be a show home, or rented accommodation. I bet the towels are even a set.'

Tom Sutherland exited the room and returned a minute later throwing a set of green towels on the floor. Ross counted three hand towels, two large towels and two even more expansive bath towels. He looked around and then it truly dawned on him.

'There's no photos. None. Either she wanted away from everything in her past or Amanda Novak was some sort of guest. For whatever reason, someone did not want her here. This place is wrong, I'm telling you. I don't know why, but something is terribly wrong here.'

Chapter 5

Macleod breathed a sigh of relief. It had taken most of the day and he had endured those breakout sessions that he hated. Back in the day, you would have sat and listened to a briefing, not undergone a whole workshop on how to use a person's first name. And besides, he was not happy with it. First names were for home, places with people you loved and cherished. But in work, a little detachment was good, reminded you that you were in a job, there to get work done, not be everyone's friend.

McGrath, of course, had no issue whatsoever with it. And maybe that was a female thing. He remembered at school that the girls had all been called by their Christian names but, at least at secondary school, he, like all the other boys, had been referred to by their surname, or at least as best they could. Often the full name was used so as not to cause confusion. So many islanders had the same surname, more so than on the mainland.

'Seoras, has Alan checked in?'

It sounded wrong but Macleod heard the same concern in Hope's voice that he felt in his own heart. Between the afternoon sessions, Macleod had been briefed by Stewart on what was happening on the Monach Islands. He had known them as abandoned stretches of land but recently a new community had settled in. If he had been in the Outer Hebrides, he may have paid more attention, but he was finding his life and his scope of interest was now becoming more Inverness-focused. That was inevitable but he could imagine the chatter about the new installation.

'I haven't had anything, Hope. I was just about to call Stewart—I mean Kirsten—before we head up the road.'

It was going to be difficult. Having to call all the team and indeed any other members of the force by their Christian name was not something he was looking forward to. And his junior officers referring to him as Seoras, not even Macleod, let alone, sir. Maybe it was time to move on. All day he had felt like some sort of dinosaur amongst the modern, cosier, sharing community he was being asked to join.

'Come on,' said Hope, 'let's grab our coats and get going. I think you've had enough change for one day.'

Macleod watched his colleague smile at him before grabbing her jacket and hauling it on. The leather suited her, and Macleod had wondered why they had not grabbed Hope as a poster face for the new police force. But he knew why. The scar that ran across her face. She had received the burn saving Macleod's partner from an acid bath but that would not matter. More important that your teeth were white and had no gaps, that your figure was trim and not obese, that your hair could sit in place. Macleod knew which type of officer he would want when he was in trouble. Battle marked and experienced would do him every time.

As the car sped out of Glasgow, Macleod called Stewart on his mobile, Hope driving as ever. 'Kirsten,' said Macleod, a little forced, 'have you heard anything more?'

'Yes,' there was a pause, 'sir. I had a call from the Sergeant on scene, a Tom Sutherland, appraising me of the names of the island inhabitants and requesting I look into the background of each. They have Wi-Fi and mobile coverage there but the weather's closing in and I think the island is becoming, if not already is, cut-off. Ross still thinks there's a possibility of murder. In fact, the Sergeant thinks that it's definite.'

'Okay, he'll need some support, soon as. I'll give him a ring.'

'And sir, are you on the way up?'

'Of course,' said Macleod, a little wearily, 'where else would I be going?'

'Don't!' said Stewart abruptly. 'The A9's closed. They have the snowploughs out but apparently it's coming down in blankets.'

'Are you suggesting I stay the night down here?'

'Probably, but I was also thinking that yourself and the Sergeant could visit the family of our victim. I've managed to trace them and I did ask for help from our colleagues in Glasgow who I believe have been around to inform the family of her death. But given the circumstances, it would be better to get a fuller picture.'

'Where are they?'

'Bridge of Weir, sir, I'll send you a grid reference and a postcode.'

'Very good, . . . Kirsten. Send along any other details you have because I think Sergeant McGrath, or rather Hope and I will need to find a hotel for the night. Might as well get caught up on the case notes.'

'Aye sir. Sending the details for the address now.'

Hope pulled the car off the road at the next junction and

41

soon they were heading back into Glasgow to then drive out to the west and the countryside beyond Glasgow. Macleod was more used to mountains and sweeping landscapes now that he was in Inverness, but not long ago he would have taken walks out in this part of the world.

The world tonight was a blanket of white, however, and the roads, a treacherous slush. Macleod filled Hope in on the details Stewart had provided and he then sat in silence pondering the night as it passed by.

'This will be Ross's first time on his own. Maybe I should give him a call directly,' said Macleod. The mobile was silent as Macleod called before it went straight to voicemail. Trying unsuccessfully a second time to get connected, Macleod left a message for Ross to call him as soon as he could.

'It's probably the weather, Seoras. I wouldn't worry.'

'I'm not worried, just concerned. The weather will make things difficult. It's not like he'll have Jona or Hazel over with him either.' The two women were the lead forensic officers in the Inverness station and Macleod had a great respect for both. They often went beyond simply feeding back detail and could be relied on when things got tough to be a source of help and inspiration.

'No, but he's got himself and whoever is with him. Alan will be fine.'

Macleod narrowed his eyes. 'You use Alan like it's your normal name for Ross. I can't get used to it.'

'It is my normal name for him,' grinned Hope. 'When you were out of action, Ross became my number two and I thought something a little more personal was appropriate, like you and me share first names.'

Macleod snorted. 'Well, that little perk's gone. All on first names now. It's too close, too much like a club and not a service.' Macleod saw Hope's shake of the head. 'It is. Trust me, it won't be a good thing.'

'Certainly not, Mr Macleod,' laughed Hope.

Bridge of Weir was a reasonably sized village in its own right, but Macleod saw it as a feeder into Glasgow. The places surrounding such large conurbations always were, but this was a more scenic one than most. The high street had the essential shops for a village of this size—takeaways, pub, convenience store. As Hope drove along, Macleod saw a car attached to a lamp post. There was no one inside it after what must have been a minor accident, but he felt completely absolved of any responsibility when he saw the police aware sticker on the side of the car.

The home of Amanda Novak's parents was hidden away in a cul-de-sac and the house had a few lights on. As Macleod stepped out of the car, he felt the crisp snow beneath him and tried to gauge where the lighter fall had been so as not to get the hems of his trousers wet. He would have put his wellington boots on but when going to a place that had suffered such bad news, he felt it might be disrespectful.

Hope rapped the door and a man with a grim face answered. He was only in his twenties, Macleod reckoned, but his face was haggard.

'DS McGrath and this is DI Macleod. We are looking to speak to the parents of Amanda Novak. Are we in the right place, sir?'

'Yes, you are, officer. I'm Derek, Amanda's brother. Our parents are inside; please come in.'

'Thank you, sir, and please accept our condolences on your loss. We'll try to make our time here as brief as possible.'

Macleod followed Hope into the house and felt the warmth of the heating straight away. As the door opened to a cosy living room, Macleod saw the family photos on the wall, two parents and two children, one male, one female.

'Mum, Dad, these are police officers; sorry, I've forgotten your names already.'

Macleod stepped forward. 'I'm DI Macleod and this is DS McGrath. We're looking into the circumstances of your daughter's death, Mr and Mrs Novak, and we would like to ask a few questions about Amanda and her recent life if that's all right. I appreciate it's a bad time but please, we would be grateful of any help you can give.'

The son offered Macleod a chair and he looked at the grieving parents, side by side on the sofa. Hands were being held and Macleod saw a balding man with a chunky face beside a similarly slightly overweight woman. They appeared to be normal parents; eyes red from tears. He hated this part of the job.

Mr and Mrs Novak, I wonder if you could tell me how Amanda got onto the Monach Islands? I know it was a new settlement but from my briefing, I understand she was not there from the start.'

The wife looked up at her husband and sniffed before the man started to speak. Each word was slow, carefully thought, or maybe it was a problem to simply say the words.

'Inspector, she simply came through one day to the house. Amanda lived along the road from us—well, at least when she was at home. Always travelling she was, a girl full of optimism and adventure. She rang us from Bangkok one time, telling us she was engaged but that never panned out. Another day we had a picture of her in front of the pyramids. We didn't even know she'd left the house.'

'So, you don't know exactly how she got the place?' clarified Macleod.

'I'm afraid not,' said Mr Novak. 'But she was delighted to go.'

'And did she take much with her?' asked Hope.

'I think she cleared the house of most things. She had stuff from all over the world due to her travels. That over there,' said the man pointing at a stuffed donkey on the mantelpiece, 'from Peru. And the shell with the dolphin coming out of it, that's Portugal. She was a club rep, position of responsibility. We were dead proud of her—who wouldn't have been. Always a free bird, our Amanda, but never unhappy, never close to . . . '

Suicide not likely thought Macleod. *Well, at least, that tallies with Ross's thinking.*

'Did she contact you much from the island?' asked Hope.

'She contacted us very rarely from anywhere. Amanda was more of an opportunist, calling on us as and when. We never wanted to be holding her back.'

'And when was the last time you spoke to Amanda?'

'Maybe two weeks ago,' said the husband. 'She was in a good mood; at least, that was what the email said.'

'So, when was the last time you actually spoke to her as opposed to email or texts?' queried Macleod.

'Oh, we only ever got emails and texts after that first month,' mused Mr Novak. 'I think we had about two calls the first month and one was to say she had arrived and that her stuff had been left behind in a depot somewhere and it was going to take a while to get it over.'

Hope continued with some clarification on these timescales, but Macleod began to watch the son. He was nervous, his face

45

shying away from his parents. It was not that he did not look upset. Just that he seemed to have an aversion to his father's description of events and of his sister.

'Perhaps your parents could do with something hot to drink,' said Macleod. 'Something for the throat, Derek. It's an awful hard thing to talk about. Maybe you could . . . '

Derek nodded and took his leave of the room and Macleod stood up. 'Sergeant McGrath will just take a few more details, Mr and Mrs Novak. I'll just give your son a wee hand if that's okay. He looks a bit strained. A terrible toll for you all.' Macleod realised he was starting to sound like the villagers he grew up amongst at local funerals. These days he was blunter, although always polite, but he felt he needed to make his escape to the kitchen seem normal.

As Macleod made his way through the living room door, he was able to see Derek Novak filling a kettle at the sink. The man turned to him and Macleod held up a hand. 'Sorry to make such an excuse but I got the distinct feeling in there that your view of your sister is not the same as your parents. I would appreciate it if I could hear your side of things, just for a more rounded view of Amanda.'

Derek said nothing until he had filled the kettle and placed it on its base and switched it on. Looking at Macleod he waited until it began to bubble and then he started in a low whisper.

'Mandy was no traveller, Inspector. My sister would have gone with a banana if it paid for the drinks and had a bit of something to throw up her nose. That's why she went everywhere. She was no responsible club rep, neither. She organised sex tours. Nothing dodgy like underage kids or forced prostitutes but actual tours for guys and that meant being available herself. I loved Mandy to bits, but she was

46

a good time girl and more. The Bangkok authorities almost lifted her for drugs, but her sponsor bribed them off because he liked her in bed.'

'And yet,' interjected Macleod, 'she took herself to a remote island to start a new life with a clean-living, eco-style commune. At least that was my take on the place.'

'If Mandy went there, she would have been after drink, drugs, or a lot of good times. Which one, I don't know but she did not fit the place you just described to me.'

'And did you hear from her after arrival?'

'Once. She manged a call to my house, telling me she loved me and a whole ton of nonsense about how we should start a business together. She was pissed or high or something. And that was that.'

'And her house here, did she keep it?'

'Oh yes, not that she ever saw it. Dad was right, it had a ton of bits and boobs from all over the world and she packed a stack to go with her.'

'Was she a tidy soul? I'm guessing no from your previous comments.'

'Mandy could make a pig embarrassed, Inspector, with the way she left her house.'

'Can you give me access to her house? I'd like to take a look around.'

Derek suddenly reared up. 'Why? They said she killed herself.'

Macleod thought about his next words but decided he should come clean with the man. 'We are treating your sister's death as suspicious. I'm not convinced she killed herself. A search of her house might give us some better idea about what she had expected on the island. There may be documentation lying around.'

'If some bastard's killed our Mandy, I'll gladly help you all I can, Inspector, but be aware, there's no rhyme nor reason to how Mandy runs her house. It could be like looking for a needle in a haystack.'

'Then I had best get to it, Mr Novak. It may be best not to say to your parents until I have a better idea of what happened. They seem to be struggling to come to terms with her death as it is.'

The man agreed and after he brought drinks through for his parents, he escorted the officers to the door. 'I don't live here so they'll maybe be expecting me to go home shortly anyway. If you wait down the road, I'll be out in about fifteen minutes. Then I'll take you to Mandy's.'

Trudging back to the car, Macleod looked over at Hope who gazed questioningly back. 'What, Seoras?'

'Amanda's brother reckoned she was a good time girl. There was no indication from the island that she was junkie or a sex addict or anything else untoward. Ross's reports only said she was quiet, kept herself to herself. Think I'll check with him.'

Macleod pulled his mobile from his pocket and called Ross's number. He stepped into the car to speak to his constable, but the call would not connect.

'Try Ross, Hope.' Macleod watched his Sergeant attempt a call three times before shaking her head. Without hesitation, he placed a call to Kirsten Stewart at the office and asked her to try all numbers onto the island. As he waited for her return call, Macleod sat tapping his feet.

'You okay, Seoras.' Macleod shook his head.

'There's something amiss here and we seem to have lost contact with our man. No, I'm not all right.'

Macleod's mobile rang and he answered it. He listened while Kirsten detailed her actions before taking the mobile down from his ear. 'Hope, there's no communications at all.'

Chapter 6

It took Derek Novak a half hour to leave his parents' house and the detectives followed his car to a cottage on the edge of the village. Snow lay on the roof and in the darkness, it was hard to see the full extent of the grounds around the building. There was a short front lawn area, but the rear seemed to have a mass of trees behind it.

Derek Novak opened the white door with a key from his jacket pocket and then flicked on light switches in the house. The building was cold and Macleod could see his breath forming in front of him.

'Does she not keep the heating going, Mr Novak? It'll be bad for the house to keep it like this.'

'Always a bare minimum of heat, that was Mandy. Meant she could spend money on other things.' There was a shake of the head to accompany the comment and Macleod felt for the brother before him. His love of his sister was clear but the disappointment he felt in how her life had gone was something he was struggling to escape.

'And where did she keep her important documents, correspondence, that sort of thing?'

'You're looking at it. Could be anywhere. She had no system, no vague place to stash bills or letters. I mean, look at it, Inspector.'

It was true. As Macleod walked from cosy sitting room to the kitchen then to the bedrooms, nothing was stowed away. There were letters strewn about the place and bits of furniture cast here and there. A blanket hung off the side of the settee with a number of letters poking out from beneath. An empty beer bottle was found lolling about under the bed, and the kitchen contained bottles of spirits poking out from behind the toaster and microwave. The place was a dump.

'Looks like we have to scan it bit by bit, sir,' said Hope.

'I respect the gesture,' said Macleod quietly to Hope, 'but I think you still have to call me Seoras in front of the general public.'

'Not sure that feels right, and I am not calling you Inspector. You'll start to think your Columbo or Morse. Think I'll use boss.'

'Whatever, Hope. But let's get on. It could take a while to get through this lot.' *And that's the problem with this whole new openness and familiarity*, thought Macleod. *The old standards were there for a reason, helped keep things professional.* 'You take the bedrooms, Hope, and I'll start in the living room and then take the kitchen. Mr Novak,' said Macleod turning to the man, 'thank you for your assistance but you really don't need to stay. I'm happy to take your key and return it to you when we are finished.'

'If you don't mind, Inspector, I'd like to stay; otherwise, it's home on my own. It's doing me good to look around here. She used to sit on that settee with her legs up, blanket over her in the winter, bottle in hand.'

'You said she engaged in a lot of . . . relationships. Was she the flirty type?'

Derek Novak almost chuckled. 'No, Inspector, anything but. I think men saw her as good looking; certainly, I know many thought her body something, but Amanda was only ever interested in what she could get out of them. Sex was a tool to use. She may have learnt that from Mother.'

Macleod thought about the older woman back at the house and struggled to understand the comment. He would come back to it if it turned out to be important at a later date. Reaching down, he picked up a stack of letters on the floor and began to scan through them. There were bills for various trips and from hotels in different parts of the world. An occasional name was written on some and Macleod showed the detail to Derek.

'Could be anyone, Inspector, certainly no one from the family. I would think these would be the people she fobbed the bills off to, or who she thought owed her for enjoying her company.'

The phrase was eloquent, but it contained a horrible image to Macleod. There was certainly nothing about this woman that screamed eco-retreat. Why on earth would she have jumped across the Minch and the far side of the Uists to a forgotten island. Did the island offer drugs, drink, or sex? Sex might be an answer but that was a stretch. Why not simply pursue these things in rather more glamourous places? The Monach Islands were probably intriguing to a lover of nature and the wilds, but it did not fit the lifestyle of this party woman.

Macleod heard a cry from the other room. It was Hope and he tore out of the living room to the claustrophobic hallway beyond and saw a figure in black reeling backwards through the bedroom door and slamming up against the hall. Hope followed, red hair flying but she was caught by a sucker punch to the stomach. The figure's crashing into the wall had done less damage to her than Hope had clearly thought.

Macleod brought himself up to a height he thought looked threatening and the figure with its green eyes scanned him for a moment. He read the contours of the body and decided it was a woman. In the past this would have given him some comfort in that he would have believed his chances of apprehending the figure would have increased. But these days, women seemed to be as strong physically, or maybe he was weakening. Certainly, the women on his team were the physically stronger part of the group.

Hope was bent double and as she rose, the woman in black kicked out at her head, catching Hope's temple, and sending her sprawling into the bedroom. Macleod advanced and as the woman turned, he saw a mass of paper in her far hand. For a moment, they stood looking at each other and Macleod realised he was the sole blockage to the front door and escape.

'What the hell?' Derek Novak must have stuck his head out of the door behind Macleod and the Inspector tried to wave him back inside with his hand. But the woman did not wait and ran down the hallway into the kitchen. Macleod, following, heard the sound of a rear door opening and then an icy blast of wind tore through the house.

'Come on, Hope,' shouted Macleod as he passed the bedroom. By the time Macleod had cleared the rear door, he could hear Hope following. Outside, he saw footprints in the snow leading to the woods behind the house. The woman was only twenty-five metres ahead and he tore out into the night after her.

The rear of the house had a large fence behind it with wire

mesh and Macleod saw the woman begin to climb it. The fence was at least ten feet high and she was clinging on as she climbed, the white papers still in her hand. Macleod thought about climbing as he reached the fence but instead decided to barrel into it with all his strength and momentum. The fence shook and the woman lost her grip, falling down. But she landed on top of Macleod. Suddenly disorientated, Macleod tried to scrabble to his feet but was pushed over in the snow.

'Seoras! I've got her, Seoras.'

Macleod looked up from his prone position to see Hope engaging the woman and the two figures tumbled together in the snow. There were punches and then he saw the woman manage to get on top of Hope. Rising to his feet, he groggily ran at the black figure now pinning Hope to the floor and jumped at her back. The woman was caught off guard and Macleod tried to wrap his arm around her neck. It slipped and he managed to grasp her balaclava as she struggled. It came free and a mass of brown hair was blown into his face by the wind. Macleod then received an elbow to the ribs that knocked him backwards.

Hope's yell of pain cut through the wind and when Macleod managed to look up, he saw the black figure now running back to the road and disappearing around the side of the cottage. His ribs ached and he felt like the wind had been knocked out of him, but he saw Hope was still lying prone. Rising, he stumbled over to her.

'Hope, you okay?'

'No,' came the resounding reply. 'That bitch can certainly punch. Is she gone?'

'Yes, Hope, she's gone. I'll call it through, but I doubt we'll be able to track her. Still, you must have got a good look at her face.'

'When?'

'When I pulled her balaclava off,' said Macleod.

'She had her thumbs in my eyes. I saw nothing. Do you mean to tell me that after all that all we got was her hair colour?'

'Well, we've narrowed it down to maybe thirty percent of the world's female population,' said Macleod. Hope looked angrily at him but then saw a smile. 'At least you're all right,' said the Inspector. 'And besides, she didn't leave us empty handed. Come on, get up. She dropped some of her sheets of paper she was carrying. Let's get them rounded up and get inside for a look.'

'Are you two okay?' asked Derek Novak on seeing the pair re-enter the house.

'Fine, Mr Novak. I don't suppose you got a look at the woman once DS McGrath had uncovered her.'

'Well, I could see she was a red head, but maybe more copper-like than a true red. Like that battery that keeps on going.' Macleod knew the one, but he had thought she was darker than that. Maybe because she was in the dark with him the hair had not shone the same.

'Did she run through the light when you saw her?'

'Yes, Inspector. I had the door open but to be honest I wasn't for running out after her. I'm not much of a fighter.'

'It's fine, Mr Novak, best left to the professionals,' said Hope.

The younger ones, thought Macleod. Making his way back into the living room, he took a coffee table and placed the papers he had gathered up from the ground and then watched Hope put her own gatherings on top. Splitting them in half, Macleod took a seat and held the second half of the papers out for his Sergeant.

'Thanks, boss. I'm going to pop out and give Kirsten a ring. If Amanda was travelling a lot, maybe Kirsten can get a track of her movements and maybe even find out who paid for her flights and that. I assume, Mr Novak,' said Hope raising her voice so the man could hear, 'that your sister would not have paid for much of her travel.'

'As little as possible.'

'Good, Hope,' nodded Macleod, 'and tell Kirsten to stay at the office. I want to do one of those video calls with her when we're done here and have found somewhere to stay.'

'Yes, boss,' and Hope disappeared outside the living room to make the call.

Macleod stared at the documents in front of him and saw various bills for electricity and gas. On another page she saw an itinerary for a trip to Dundee. There was a two-night stay in The Regency Hotel and Macleod made a note to get that checked out. Another piece of paper showed an invoice for a trip to Mauritius and attached to it was a photograph. The image showed Amanda Novak in bikini bottoms and nothing else standing in the surf. Turning the photograph over Macleod saw a signature and read the caption, 'Your Gomez, to my Morticia'. A little weird. Macleod handed the photograph to Derek Novak, coughing before saying, 'Apologies for the image but do you recognise this photograph or any of the writing on the back? Does the reference to the Adams family mean anything to you?'

'Only that she loved the show as a kid, Inspector. But this image, that's Amanda, I'm sad to say. No shame, no care, using whatever she could to get what she wanted.'

That's a little harsh, thought Macleod, *but maybe he knows her best. Nothing wrong with the image in its proper context. Among lovers, not a problem. And there are beaches like that.* At least that was what Macleod had been told. Hope would be a better informant about sunning yourself in the warmer parts of the world.

Macleod checked the remainder of his documents and found nothing unusual. When Hope returned, he handed her the itineraries and the photograph.

'Snap. I got one of those as well,' she said handing a photograph to Macleod. The image was similar, identical bikini bottoms but this was indoors, in front of a large swimming pool. Given Miss Novak's lack of clothing and the fact there were no other bathers behind her, Macleod assumed it was a private pool. On turning the photograph over he saw once again the signature 'Gomez'.

'There's a line of enquiry, boss. I'll get Stewart to run an alias check and see if we can't figure out who Gomez is. She certainly appears close to him. I couldn't see anything else, but I guess the Dundee trip is worth following up. There's no mention of Gomez on it.'

Macleod stretched his back and stifled a yawn. The dead woman's brother was still in the room and a show of fatigue might not be the best thing at the moment. 'I guess we had better check every other paper in here before we go,' said Macleod and took a handful off the floor scanning through them.

Two hours later, Macleod watched Derek Nova lock up the house and realised that it was already ten o'clock and they still had nowhere to stay. Waving goodbye to Mr Novak, Macleod watched the snow begin to fall again, even heavier than before.

'Let's go and check in somewhere before we make our call to Kirsten. I think we should go to the airport in case we need to get over to Uist in a hurry tomorrow.'

'How do the flights work?' asked Hope.

'Well, you need to go from Glasgow and then catch the Barra flight which hops on to Benbecula. Although I think there is a direct service, too. Not many times a day mind, maybe once or twice. Then we'll need to get a car and drive down to the shore and find someone with a boat to take us out to the Monachs. With the wild weather it won't be easy.'

Hope nodded. 'Kirsten said Jona had looked into getting over to help Lucy, but it was a no go due to weather. A rough swell and she got an absolute no from everyone.'

'If things get worse, do we have a back-up plan to get there?' asked Macleod.

'I guess we could ask a lifeboat or a helicopter, but you'll need to be desperate to get them to fly in this weather.'

Stepping into the car, Macleod sat thoughtfully as Hope started it. Ross was on his own with a murderer on an island of so few people. At this time there was no communications with the island. When should he become worried? The weather was getting the blame at the moment but how long should he allow his junior officer to be out of contact. A hand touched his.

'Alan will be all right, Seoras. You know what we say—Ross has it covered, everything. He's thorough and not a risk taker.'

'I know, Hope, but it doesn't make it any easier when you're sat in the dark.'

Chapter 7

Ross poured the hot water from the kettle into his cup and watched the brown grains become a black liquid. The brand of coffee was not one he particularly enjoyed but after being out in the storm, he was keen to have something warm inside him. His two male colleagues were sitting down on chairs attempting to call their families at home and from the look of it they were not having any success.

'It's still down, Ross. I can't make any headway at all.' Tom Sutherland swore and then got to his feet as if there was something he could do about the situation.

'Here,' said Ross, offering the man a cup of steaming coffee, 'get that down you and we'll have a bit of a think about what to do.' Lucy was behind her screens working on the corpse of Amanda Novak, although Ross was unsure how much the woman could achieve without a proper mortuary or laboratory for tests. Grabbing another cup, Ross handed it to the shivering hands of John Allen. The man had been standing outside with Lucy and the cold had gotten to him. With the time at ten o'clock, it was probably best if John warmed up and got some sleep.

'Lucy, got your drink here,' shouted Ross over the top of the screens.

'Okay, I'm coming,' came the indignant reply. Once again, Ross felt like he had in some way annoyed the woman, but she emerged from behind the screen in her coverall without a smile or any sort of greeting at all. Her face said nothing, no annoyance, no anger, just nothing.

With the small party all seated in a circle on simple wooden stools, Ross felt like he was in a youth group gathering, or maybe Sunday School where he was about to enlighten the others. The hall was moderately warm, certainly better than outside but the when the wind blew against the windows and the door, or howled around the corners, you felt a chill inside.

The faces before him looked tired. The two men had been here from early on and Lucy had travelled, like Ross, from some distance, so fatigue was certainly setting in.

'I thought it best to gather and collect some thoughts before deciding the next course of action. As you know, the lines of communication with the mainland have gone. My colleagues are investigating but without being able to speak to them it's difficult to know what my Inspector would want. What he would want, and I'm sure it's something we would all do anyway, is to push forward the investigation and so with that in mind, I want to see the residents from the other two islands tomorrow.

'Amanda Novak was certainly killed and then set up to look like a suicide. So far, I've kept our tone to the residents easy going as if nothing is overly wrong. I'm aware we are on our own here and well, let's say that is not a great position with a killer on the loose. But with the weather as it is, I think it best we bunker down in this hall for the night and resume if we can in the morning.'

Ross watched the faces of those around him and realised he was not going to get any argument from them. He watched Lucy shiver slightly as she drank from her cup, her face looking sombre, somewhat distant. What was running around her head was anyone's guess, but he realised he needed to watch his team.

Yes, it was his team, was it not? It was an unusual situation and not one Ross had contemplated when he had risen that morning for work. As the junior in his own team, Ross was always running here and there, making sure everything was set up correctly, that the mechanics of investigation rolled on while his bosses tended to do a lot of the thinking and directing. Now it was Ross about to do that. But first, this team needed a rest.

'We do have evidence in this hall,' said Ross, 'and that is why I intend to keep it guarded. So, we shall go on a guard rotation of four hours at a time through the night. I'll take the first four hours and then Tom you can take over. John, sleep through until six. If our communications get re-established, then send through a report of all that's happened and ask for support ASAP.

'We need to stay cautious so as of now we always go in pairs. There's something hidden here, someone is not who they are pretending to be, and with so few of us, I think we need to be coy and watchful. Any questions?'

The only response was a weary shake of the head from Tom Sutherland. As his team retired to the mattresses that had been provided for them, Ross checked the entrances to the hall, making sure they were locked. He did not know if all the keys had been given to him, so he blocked the two side doors with fold up tables. At the very least they would make an almighty clatter if anyone came in that way.

With all his team under blankets and attempting to sleep, Ross switched the lights out and sat in the dark of the hall. The wind howled outside and he watched more snow fall. Whether it was this sight or his actual temperature dropping, Ross was unsure, but he found himself grabbing some of his own blankets and wrapping himself up as he took his turn on watch.

For two hours Ross stared at the weather outside, letting the thoughts of the day slowly run through his head. He watched faces from the island appear and blend before him, replaying snippets of conversation. His mind wandered back to Kirsten in the office, wondering if she would still be there, glasses pressed onto her nose and eyes wandering across any information her computer could garner.

The Inspector would be champing at the bit. The thought of the man stranded and awaiting a plane or boat to carry him over here made Ross smile. The man was a dinosaur in a lot of ways and the way he tacitly tried to avoid conversation about Ross's partner made him smile. Ross always found it funny. Macleod reckoned Ross had made a choice to find men attractive. Some of his friends would get upset about that but it was not Ross's nature. Instead, he was thankful, thankful that Macleod was trying, ham-fisted as it was, and that he did not live some fifty years ago when it would have been a different story.

Something stirred behind him and turning he saw Lucy rise up from her mattress and wander towards him still wrapped in her blankets. Ross was about to offer a drink when the woman without any warning plonked herself right onto his lap.

'Wrap us up.'

She had simply muttered the words and her eyes were now shut. Ross was a little put out. This was hardly appropriate behaviour and he wondered what she was doing. His sexuality was well-known, so surely, she could not be coming from that angle.

'Cold. Wrap us up.'

Taking Lucy at her word, Ross wrapped a blanket around her, and the woman laid her head on his shoulder. Within a minute, he could hear light snoring and contented himself that the next two hours of his watch would be done holding onto this sleeping figure.

There was a noise outside. It was a definite thump of some sort and loud enough to heard above the wind. Ross glanced towards the door of the hall, but nothing stirred. He wondered if they were being watched. Since working with Macleod, Ross had become much more suspicious of people and situations, probably a good thing in a detective. The Inspector had on numerous occasions used his distrust of people's intentions to open up other angles on cases. And in truth, it was these lessons he had received that had him wanting to keep the islanders at bay tonight.

Rather than move and check what had made the sound, Ross stayed still and tried to pretend he was asleep as well. If anyone was watching, whether through the windows, or from a hidden camera, then they would see nothing but a sleeping party of investigators.

The wind continued and the endless fall of snow followed. After the loud noise, everything had seemed to go back to normal and Ross wondered if something had happened. Some part of a house coming off, a roof tile maybe. But then again there were no tiles on these roofs. And then Ross thought he saw something orange flickering in the distance towards the homes of the islanders.

Ross tapped Lucy's shoulder. 'Get up, Lucy, get up.' The orange glow started to become more intense. 'Lucy, get up!'

'What? No, cold, sleeping.'

'Up!' shouted Ross, standing and Lucy fell to the floor. Not looking at her, Ross stared as the orange glow now began to flicker at the top. His stomach sank as he realised he was looking at a fire. 'Tom, John, up! Get up! Everyone!'

Ross tore to the door and opened it into a wind that had not subsided during the night. His foot stepped into three inches of snow and he felt the cold at his ankles. But the flames he had seen a moment ago were now higher, much higher. Turning back inside, he ran for his coat.

'John, Lucy, stay and lock the door behind us. Tom, you're with me. One of the houses is on fire.'

'Fire? Oh, bloody hell!' With that, Tom was running for his own jacket, throwing on his stab vest first as an automatic response. But Ross was not waiting and raced out of the door and into the deep snow. His breath filled the air before him as he puffed hard cresting the small rise up to the village square. By now he could feel the heat and saw the Mayor standing before the burning house along with most of the village.

Orla McIlroy was in a state, screaming incoherently and Alfie Collins was showing her no quarter as he slapped her across the face, telling the woman to be quiet. The wind howled and the sight was surreal as the house burned with an intense heat, but the snow still blustered across their faces.

'Kiera!' yelled Orla. 'Come back, Kiera! I said come back, he's not worth it!'

Ross ran up to the Mayor and grabbed his arm. 'Is there

someone in there?' Ross pointed and then recoiled as something exploded inside the house. It wasn't that the flames came any closer, but the noise of the explosion even drowned out the wind momentarily.

'I don't think so. We need to do a headcount.'

'Tom,' shouted Ross over the wind and confusion, 'get a headcount of the villagers. And do it quick; there might be someone in there.'

Tom Sutherland immediately started running up to people and faces. There was Daniella in a large dressing gown with Paul Kemp in pyjama bottoms and a large coat before her. Alfie Collins was still chastising Orla McIlroy. And there was the Mayor, his own daughter well behind him. Edna, where was Edna Collins? Tom Sutherland spun around and then saw a face at the window of one of the houses. The old woman was watching intently, safe behind a pane of glass. But Tom saw no Kiera Harris. Young and somewhat flirtatious, it was hard to forget her. But she was nowhere in sight.

'I can't see Kiera Harris, Ross. The young girl's missing.'

Ross ran up to Orla McIlroy who was receiving another slap across the face with the verbal command of 'calm down!'

'Get out of the way, Mr Collins,' shouted Ross and shoved the man hard, causing him to fall into the snow. 'Orla, where's Kiera. Where has Kiera gone?' The woman simply burst into tears. 'Is she in there?' Ross asked in a clear and deliberate tone. The woman jerked and shuddered as she nodded her head.

'Tom, Kiera's in there. I'm going in. Keep everyone safe and see if you can get some fire defences sorted.'

Without waiting for an acknowledgement, Ross ran to the open door of the house. The glass had shattered from the heat of the fire and while the frame was still intact, he could simply walk through where the large pane of glass had been.

Inside the hall, the carpet was burning and Ross pulled his coat around him. 'Kiera! Are you there, Kiera?' Ross kicked open the door of the living room and jumped back as a blast of heat and flame poured out. After standing clear, Ross entered and saw the sofa ablaze. It was then that it dawned on him whose house he was in. This was Amanda Novak's abode on the island. With the rush to the fire, he had not clocked the house he was attending, instead more concerned by the thought that someone could be in trouble.

Regardless of whose house it was and what damage was being done to evidence, Ross needed to find the woman whose life was still at risk. 'Kiera! Kiera!' He tried to get into the kitchen from the hall, but the door handle was roasting hot and every kick he gave the door failed to force it open. Returning to the living room, he saw a wooden chair and picked it up. It was a solid build, not a cheap imitation, and Ross re-entered the hallway with it. From one end he made the five-step charge to the kitchen door and stumbled as it gave way on impact. The chair went from his grasp, he fell to the floor and felt a surge of heat overhead.

Pulling himself to his feet, Ross once more wrapped his coat around him and entered the kitchen. As he stepped in, something crashed down from above, barely missing him and causing him to run into the corner of the petite kitchen. From the corner of his eye, he saw the hair of a woman, long and splayed out. Quickly, Ross reached for her and grabbing her shoulders pulled her towards him. The woman was lifeless, but he simply threw her over his shoulder. But he saw underneath her was another body and a face he had not seen before.

Ross could not take both of them at once. There was no decision to make; he would need to make a return trip. Turning to the door of the kitchen, he stepped across the burning material that had fallen and ran down the hallway, jumping through the open pane of the front door. The woman's feet must have caught on the door because she started to slip off his shoulder and he stumbled before landing in the snow. The unconscious woman landed beside him.

'Tom, see what you can do with this one.' Ross pushed himself back up and turned to the house.

'Where are you going?' shouted Tom as he slid to his knees beside the recently deposited figure.

'There's one more in there. I need to go back.'

As Ross began to walk back to the house, he was grabbed by the arm. 'Don't be foolish, man. You got one, be glad of that. You'll die this time.'

'Get off—there's one more in there.'

'Don't be daft. Your Sergeant counted us all, there was only young Kiera missing and you have brought her back to us. You must have seen something that looked like a person. I won't let you go.'

Ross felt his other arm being grabbed and saw Alfie Collins grabbing him as well. The older man was not strong and Ross shook his hand from the arm. But the Mayor grabbed Ross all the tighter to the point that he was actually pulling Ross away.

'Let go, sir, or I will be forced to take action.' Ross gave the man three seconds and then shoved him hard, causing him to stumble back and fall over into the snow. Without looking back, he plunged back through the open door.

The fire was as intense if not more so, but he knew his route. As he reached the kitchen, he heard a popping sound, like rapid gunfire of sorts but on a quieter scale. As he stepped over the flaming piece of debris on the floor, he heard more pops and something hit his cheek at pace.

The popping was coming from across the kitchen just above the figure on the floor. As Ross quickly got closer, his coat and hands shielding his face, he saw the bag of popcorn from between his fingers. Ignoring it and reaching down, he dragged the figure up by the shoulders. The face was heavily burnt and Ross smelt something like petrol. The figure was not burning, but it was lifeless.

Hoisting it over his shoulder, he felt a more considerable weight this time. Or was he suffering from smoke inhalation. Either way he needed to get out. Across from him another piece of ceiling fell and flames whipped past his face. He was trapped by this burning pile of debris, cornered in the kitchen. Ross made a decision and simply walked over the debris and felt a pain shoot around his legs. As he reached the hallway, he knew he was on fire and started to run as best he could. Falling out of the door, he let his burden fall from his shoulders as he tumbled into the snow. Within seconds he could hear Tom Sutherland speaking, reassuring and calm. Snow was being packed around him and he felt burning hot and ice cold across his body all at once.

'You'll be fine Ross, just a bit of fire. Well done, man, well done. You got him. Whoever he is!'

Chapter 8

Ross lay back on the snow, his heart pounding but the pain of the fire on his leg was gone. Instead, he began to feel cold. A blanket was thrown over him and Tom Sutherland moved away to be replaced by Autumn Forester. The teenager said nothing, but rubbed Ross's face with her hand, staring, compassionate eyes boring into his soul. He tried to move but she pushed him back down, quite forcibly for her age, and produced a small bottle. Carefully she let him take a sip before running her hands across his cheek again.

'Bugger it!' It was Sergeant Sutherland's voice and Ross knew by the anguish in it that someone had not made it out of the fire. Much to Autumn's silent objections, Ross raised himself up to a sitting position and watched Tom Sutherland checking the pulse of the figure Ross had extricated from the building.

'Sergeant, is he?'

'I doubt he was alive when you picked him up. I believe it's a he, but to be honest, he's too badly burnt. There's also a whiff of petrol.' Sutherland stood up and rounded on the mayor. 'Is there anyone on this island you haven't told us about? Anyone stopping by or who pops on occasionally? Answer me, man.'

The mayor reeled. Something seemed to be dawning on him but the mayor was reluctant to believe it. 'We have a boy that size on the other island. One of the Arnolds, Alan. But they are on Shivinish. He wouldn't have come across in this weather.'

'Anyone here seen him? Anyone?' shouted the Sergeant above the wind. The man was becoming overwrought, yelling at everyone like that. Maybe it was shock. How many times did the everyday policeman find or see a body? Ross was used to it, too used to it, and he had methods of dealing with the blackness that came with this sort of work. But Sutherland was beginning to lose it.

'Sergeant, help me to my feet, please.' Ross was gently spoken by nature but when he needed a colleague to do something or he wanted the attention of a room, he could change that tone to one that struck fear into others. But his face usually struggled to back up this effect. But Sergeant Sutherland was in no doubt that Ross expected him to get into line despite Ross being the junior officer.

The Sergeant came over and pulled Ross up. 'Easy, Tom,' Ross whispered into his ear, 'we still have a fire, and we need to get Kiera Harris to Lucy.' Having regained his feet, Ross loudly announced to Sergeant Sutherland that he was to take Kiera Harris down to the Community Hall where Lucy could attend to her. 'And let no one else in,' whispered Ross as he feigned a hug for his colleague.

With Tom carrying Kiera down to the hall, Ross realised he was now alone, something he requested none of the others do, but he had the company of others. Orla McIlroy tore off after Tom Sutherland as he left but the mayor stood and looked at the burning building.

'Do we have anything to fight this fire with? Surely you

made provisions for such an incident?'

The mayor stared blankly at Ross for a moment, still shell-shocked, before pointing to something at the rear of his house. Autumn Forester raced off and Ross followed her to a wooden hut behind the house. The girl flung open the doors and Ross saw a stacked unit with many items he had difficulty seeing in the dark. Before he could investigate, Autumn threw him a fire hose and then a second one. The girl grabbed a metal pipe and some sort of large turnkey before running back towards the village square. Paul Kemp was kneeling on the ground and he gratefully took the pipe from Autumn, fixing it into a hole in the ground. Quickly he used the turnkey and Ross saw a fast flow of water leaving the end of the pipe. Kemp shut the valve again and then took the end of Ross's length of hose. Rather than wait, Ross made his way across the square and held the hose end towards the house, bracing himself.

Water flew from the hose end and Ross fought to hold it steady. Then someone came up behind him and placed two hands on the hose. 'Leave it, I have it. I used to be a fireman so I know what I'm doing.'

Ross stepped away at Paul Kemp's instruction and watched the man start to direct the hose to particular spots in the house. Daniella stood at a distance waving her arms about, shouting at Paul, but the man was paying her no attention. Alfie Collins had wandered off and Ross could see him back inside his house, watching with an arm around his wife.

'This is madness, detective. What on earth? This can't happen in a place like this. One person, dear Amanda killing herself, but this lad whoever he is. And Kiera, why Kiera?'

'Mayor Forester, I realise it's a shock, but you need to stay calm. I'll stay out here with Mr Kemp. Maybe Autumn could take you inside and get you something to steady your nerves. This may take a while to burn out. It's a good job there's such a distance between the houses or the whole lot might have gone up.'

'Designed that way. It was designed that way. It's the wood. We can't even call for help, terrible. We lost the communications; do you hear? We lost them.'

Ross struggled to believe the man's agitation but neither did he have time to deal with the mayor at the moment. Kemp was doing well but this fire was going to blaze for a while.

'Autumn, take your father inside. I'll come see him when I get a chance.' In the midst of the chaos, Autumn gave Ross a smile, brief but warm and then took her father's hand. One issue down but plenty more to come.

It was five in the morning when the water for the hose ran out but at that point Kemp stated that the fire was under control and would simply burn out of its own accord. Ross looked at the embers of a house and felt cold. For the last two hours he had a personal bonfire before his face but now with the flames having died down, he felt that wind bite into him.

'If you're okay, Mr Kemp, I'd like to see the Sergeant and my team before returning to the mayor. You have done a good job, sir. I'd have been lost to know how to do it.'

'All about seeing the fire for what it is, detective. Also, fortunate that the house was not that large. I hope you got anything you needed from the house yesterday because I doubt that there will be much left.'

Very convenient for someone, thought Ross but his face showed no rancour. Instead he smiled at Kemp, a grin that said he had got plenty the day before. Trudging back towards the community hall, he saw the lights on, and knocked at the

72

door when he realised his request for locked doors had been observed.

'Ross, is it out yet?' asked Sutherland opening the door to him.

'All but, Sergeant. Is Orla McIlroy here?' Tom Sutherland nodded.

'I was going to say no but she is her partner, so it would seem a bit strange. But we haven't left her alone anywhere. Lucy tended to Kiera who's asleep. She has burns but Lucy felt they were minor, or at least not life threatening. However, our victim is seriously burnt, almost unrecognisable.'

'Let's hope there's something of him for Lucy to work with.'

The Sergeant nodded and shouted at Constable Allen to get Ross a cup of something hot. The heat of the room almost made Ross swoon but then he realised he was also starving and sought some biscuits. With a sugar rush ingested, he took up a seat beside Orla McIlroy who simply stared at the sleeping Kiera Harris.

'She's alive. If we can get the communications network running, we can get her off to the hospital with the helicopter.'

Orla nodded but did not turn to face Ross. He sat in silence wondering if he should give this woman some space at this unholy hour of the morning but then he thought about Macleod. He would not sit back, would not refrain from finding out what was going on.

'Orla, what was Kiera doing in that house?'

'What? She saw it go on fire. Ran from our bed and raced to it.'

'But why go inside?'

'I don't know. Maybe she saw someone, maybe there were cries. I'm afraid I did not move so quick.'

Ross looked at Kiera Harris as she slept and noted she was in a jumper. He stood up and walked over to Sergeant Sutherland. 'Tom, what was Kiera wearing when you brought her in here.'

'What she has on, Ross. Lucy cut her coat away before placing the bandages on but she's in what she had on. Lucy said it was for the best. I think she wants her evacuated tomorrow. Sorry, today. As soon as we get the comms going.' The man dipped his head and then said,' Sorry, Ross. Started to lose it up there. Feels like someone's killing people off. Almost at will.'

'Tom, I think they are. And that's why we need to keep it tight and sensible. I fully expect back-up to arrive today at some point. But until then, we stay in pairs and we investigate. Something is not right in this place and I intend to hand the solution to my boss when he arrives.'

'You work for Macleod, don't you? He's the one pissed off everyone up the chain over those killings on the west coast. Told them all what was going on and they didn't believe him. They say he's a grumpy shit too, hard line Presbyterian.'

'Well, he has a gay and two women on his team so maybe he's mellowing.' As a defence of his boss, it was pretty crude, but Ross felt a loyalty to his Inspector and no one got to paint an ill picture of him. Hope would have told the man to . . . well, go away, but that sort of language was not in Ross.

Walking away abruptly, Ross made for the screens covering the impromptu morgue they had set up at the far end of the room. Ross had just spent hours beside a fire and the smell of it was now a background norm but as he rounded the screens his nose detected a new and darker taint to this tapestry. The charred flesh of the figure on the table was smelt before Ross saw it and it jarred him. Sure, he had carried the man out but that was in the heat of the moment and although he remembered smelling what he thought was petrol from the corpse, he had no time to inhale and think about what had happened. But now in the quiet of the hall, Ross took in the horror of the actions visited on this man. Had he been alive when he was doused? Had he been conscious?

Lucy was at another table looking closely at something. 'Don't touch anything. You might contaminate it.' It was not a rebuke. Ross was in the force many years now and was no amateur around the mortuary but rather it was simple statement of fact. 'You're going to ask how it happened?'

'And you're going to tell me quietly, we have an injured party on the other side of the screen, and possible suspects, so let's keep it quiet.'

'Of course, Ross.' Lucy made the statement as if Ross were stating the obvious, delivering the words in a cold and detached way. One could not have made the connection to the woman who had climbed onto his knee to try and stay warm earlier.

'Was he alive when he was burning?'

'Yes, as best I can tell. There are lines around his wrists and ankles where the skin is burnt differently. He was certainly bound, and I can find no other mode of death. That being said, it is a rather cursory inspection. I don't have many tools to work with.'

'And,' Ross sniffed involuntarily, 'was it petrol?'

'That's definitely the smell. If I can get access to the house, I can tell you if that's how they started it.'

'Not for now, the last embers are still being put out. We'll wait a bit for that. Besides there's not much left.'

'It'll still be worth going over,' said Lucy, flatly. 'I couldn't find anything in his clothing. Not surprising really, there's none left. Truly little really. I would say he had a large sports coat on, I found the zip and the small pieces of remaining fabric look like one of those waterproof jackets. There's bits of underwear and t-shirt burnt in with the flesh. I'm scavenging what I can, but they did a good job. There won't be much to find on this body. But let's search the house, or what's left of it.'

Ross looked away from the body and took a breath. He was exhausted, having had no sleep that night. Part of him wanted to rest but he needed to visit the house again and secure it. There was also the family on the other island to see when the tides and weather allowed. And he needed to do that while keeping his team safe. With two dead, Ross realised the team were in serious jeopardy.

Stop running scared, he chastised himself. *Macleod would never run scared. Keep them safe but let's get investigating. Kiera Harris nearly died—why? Orla might know something; I certainly don't believe her story. More so I need someone here to prevent the two women making a story up when Kiera awakes. I'm too stretched. We need to get communications running.*

Chapter 9

Macleod ended the call on his mobile and sighed. Hope would be here in a moment and they would tie up with Stewart in Inverness. Macleod had barely sat down when he had called Jane to advise that he would not be making it home tonight. Although not a regular occurrence, Jane was used to the sudden overnight stays and the losing of her partner for days at a time when a case took over. Although she had not said so, he could hear the disappointment in her voice.

The worst part of it all was that he was overtired. He knew that once he had concluded their online meeting, he would struggle to sleep and then would not be refreshed for whatever plane he could catch in the morning. And he had no clothes to change into. The conference in Glasgow was meant to have been a quick trip. Hope had picked him up at five in the morning and they would be racing back up the A9 to Inverness in the dark. Not anymore.

There was a knock at the door and he opened it to see his colleague. The ponytail Hope wore when on duty was gone and her red hair swung as she plonked herself in a chair before the hotel room's table.

'Have you got your laptop, Hope? You set up the meeting. You know how much I hate these things. You always work them better.'

'Of course, Seoras. And don't forget our new protocols around how we address our colleagues.'

'How could I forget? I had eight hours of that relentless man preaching at us today. You think someone could have started this case about a day earlier and I could have been saved from his incessant cheeriness.'

Macleod would never speak to any other colleague like this. To everyone else, he would talk of a policy change and how they would all have to adapt to the more informal tone colleagues were to have with each other. But with Hope, he said what he felt. They were incredibly open with each other these days. But then again, they were now more friends than colleagues.

Macleod saw Hope wince as she opened the laptop. 'Are you okay?'

'Just sore where that woman clocked me. It's the shoulder that was caught. Whoever she was, she knew how to punch but she was not looking to knock me out. Just fight me off so she could run.'

'No panic from her?' asked Macleod and he stood behind Hope and began to place a hand on her sore shoulder.

'Exactly. Oh, that's good—just rub that for a moment.

Macleod was focused on Hope's shoulder and he worked it this way and that to try and relieve its tightness, but he stopped abruptly when he heard the call connecting on her laptop to the Inverness officer. By the time Kirsten Stewart appeared on screen, her thick glasses occupying most of the screen, Macleod was sitting on the bed a discrete distance from Hope.

'Kirsten,' said Hope, 'how are you getting along?'

'Hello, boss, and sir, almost didn't see you.'

'You didn't get the memo sent out today then,' said Macleod.

'Oh, I did, but I wasn't too sure how you would feel about it.' Stewart looked like a rabbit in the headlights.

'I feel about it like I feel about all policy; it is what it is so there'll be no more Stewart, it's Kirsten from now on. And I guess you call me Seoras.' Stewart remained silent. 'Did you hear me, Kirsten. Hope, is that screen frozen?'

'The screen's fine, boss. It's just Kirsten that's frozen.'

'Sorry, sir, but I can't call you Seoras; after all, you are the DI.' Stewart looked down at her desk and Macleod felt the awkwardness. That was the problem with these people who dreamt up policy. You don't become closer by the names you use. Even if he referred to Kirsten as Miss Stewart, he would be as close as he was now.

'So, what name am I to have, Kirsten? I take it you are okay with me calling you by your Christian name?'

'Yes, sir.'

'And Hope's your boss too, so what are you going to call her?' asked Macleod.

'Probably boss.'

Hope began to laugh but Macleod saw no point for hilarity about this; it was, after all, a point of policy. 'You have anything sensible to offer, Hope, rather than just laughing at us.'

'Quite simple, sir.' Macleod rolled his eyes. 'I think we should address each other by first names, except I think you should be *boss* when the time is right. That do you, Kirsten? Boss?'

'And how should we address you, Hope?'

'Hope, always Hope, unless you're comfortable with *Your Highness*.' Stewart laughed and Macleod saw that Hope had broken the tension in her usual impolite way. 'Now that's done, can we get on with the case? Kirsten, what do you have?' asked Hope.

'Okay, well first off, looking at the documents that you sent me, I have found travel details for Amanda Novak travelling to Mauritius last year with a John Bonnar. Mr Bonnar paid and I have a credit card account for him but tracing it any further becomes difficult. I tried tracing her passport as well and tied in that credit card account to another four trips over the previous two years. Incidentally, the stay at the Regency was paid for by Mr Bonnar too. In fact, it was for a double suite so he may have stayed there.'

'But you don't know who this man is?' asked Macleod. 'Do you have anything on him at all?'

'No, sir,—sorry, boss. I was thinking someone should visit the Regency and see if anyone there remembers them. Long shot but worth a look. I could run over tomorrow.'

'Good idea, Kirsten, but let's get through all we know before we make any plans. What do you know about the rest of the group on the island?'

'From the top then, Mayor Duncan Forester. Widowed four years ago. Lived in Glasgow for a large number of years, several addresses, initially starting in quite poor estates before moving out to the suburbs. Worked as a consultant to Kimble Construction but I can't find out why he's a consultant. He doesn't seem to have any noted experience in that field. His daughter attended some rather decent schools, mainly boarding away. Very pricey, especially in the days before his consultancy work.'

'Money from elsewhere,' said Hope, 'but why end up on an island village that's meant to be about a simpler way of life. Seems a sudden jump.'

'Kimble Construction, Kirsten,' interrupted Macleod, 'who and how much money? Get into that.'

'I thought you would never ask, boss. Doing rather well for themselves, posted a profit over the last ten years which has grown, almost doubling every year. Also tagged by the drugs squad as a possible money laundering outfit.'

Macleod stood up off the bed and then realised he was now presenting a view of his stomach to Kirsten. Sitting back down, he saw the corner of her mouth curl up. *Blasted technology!*

'Good, Kirsten, definitely a line to pursue there. Who's next?'

'Alfie and Edna Collins, boss. A couple who, for the most part, are working for legitimate chemists and pharmaceutical companies. Alfie's a chemical engineer and his wife a pharmacist or chemist. She's harder to tie down in terms of specific job as she floats between the two. Both Glasgow natives and have not left the country in over fifty years. I can't find anything unusual in the life or accounts. Everything normal and above board. Both in the later part of life and technically retired two years ago and then ran off to the Monach Islands. Couple looking for a quiet life perhaps?'

'Well, that didn't work out,' said Hope. 'Who else do we have?'

'An Orla McIlroy, from Northern Ireland but been in Glasgow since university. Also, a chemist, but has not had any real employment as far as I can tell?'

'Then why's she a chemist?' asked Hope.

'Because she holds a first-class degree in the subject from Glasgow University. Not a lot else to say either. Two dead parents, father died in some dissident trouble back in the province and the mother passed away two years ago. Why she's there, I can't say.'

'Right then, so the mayor's looking good at the moment. Who else, Kirsten?'

'Kiera Harris, another Irish native who went to Glasgow. She has no qualifications and was once picked up in a raid for people trafficking. Turns out it was a brothel house, and the women weren't trafficked, but it was certainly not a clean place. Drugs found but Kiera was not implicated in anything. There's little else on her. No bank accounts or that. No photographs either but the name tagged.'

'No bank? That's different, don't you think, boss? The rest are a bit classier than her; how did she get her way onto the island?'

'Indeed,' replied Macleod. 'Is that it, Kirsten?'

'No, saving the best until last. Married couple Daniella White and Paul Kemp. Only married three years ago and before that they used to be in warehouse distribution and finance. Daniella used to be Daniel and as far as I can gather that changed about five years ago but I don't have any reasons as to why.'

'Probably a good thing Ross is there then, Seoras, and not you,' laughed Hope.

'Enough! And it's boss, remember.' Macleod kept a serious face, but he took the tease in a good way. It was true he was not the modern man of the team but he wished he were there. Something inside was giving him real concern for Ross.

'Paul Kemp was also a firefighter in his younger days before he got into warehousing. And this is the interesting bit. He worked for Smithton Packaging, a subsidiary of Kimble holdings who also own Kimble Construction.'

'Now, that is interesting,' noted Hope.

'Oh, there's more. Daniella used to work for Tarot Finance

and guess who they are a subsidiary of.'

'Nice work, Kirsten. So—'

'Hang on, sir—two more groups to tell you about. There's the Arnolds, a family of six, parents are David and June. He's a fisherman and there's little else on them. Certainly, no connection with anyone else there I can find. And lastly Celeste Dubois and Hamish MacArthur. She came over to Scotland five years ago and studied at Glasgow University. He was a boatman on the Clyde for most of his life. They had joint council tax three years ago and now they are on the island. But I can't tie them to any holdings.'

'That's a right patchwork of people, Kirsten, but this common link to Kimble Holdings interests me. Do you know who is on the board or runs that company?'

'Now that's the really interesting part. It's Viscount Donoghue, the owner of Morning Light and a prominent businessman who seems to have rallied well after a serious decline in fortunes some twenty years ago. Although he keeps himself to himself, he certainly has moved up in lifestyle and now has a small estate just north of Perth as well as a town house in Glasgow.'

'That sounds promising,' murmured Hope.

'Maybe, but he's as clean as a whistle. Even the HMRC can't put a finger on him.'

'That's a lot of people and it's hard to see the interaction without being there. Priority is communication with Ross or to get over there. So, in the morning if we haven't heard anything, I'll start making my way over there, though I don't know how exactly. Kirsten, get down to Dundee and the Regency. See what they know, if anything. Then I want you to go and see Viscount Donoghue. Tell him the bad news and

83

see how he takes it. I want you to look for the links in his businesses and for anything unusual.

'Hope, I want you to get into Amanda Novak's life and hunt down who she mixed with. We have a few details but not much. I want to know why someone on a new lifestyle island is killed and made to look like suicide. Was she in trouble from off-island? Was one of her suitors unhappy at her disappearing to there? Did she owe money? Somebody was close to her given the photographs we've seen. Someone paid for trips.

'So that's three lines to follow. Viscount Donoghue and company connections of the people. Amanda Novak's life and suitors. And the interaction on the island. Happy?'

'Yes, sir,' answered Kirsten. 'Sorry, force of habit. I'll let you get to bed as I'll have an early start in the weather tomorrow. 'Night, boss, Hope.'

Stewart disappeared from the screen and Hope closed down the laptop. Picking it up, she stood up to go to the door but then saw Macleod looking out of his hotel window at a snowy runway and terminal building. Unusually for the airport, there was little noise in the sky although the place still seemed to be beavering away on the ground.

'You're worried about him?'

'Ross? Aye, that I am, Hope.'

'I told you he's a good officer. Thorough and cautious, more so than me, he'll be all right.'

'Chemical engineer, pharmacist, chemist, distribution, boat-man and a manager over the top. Sounds like a lovely place to make your product away from prying eyes.'

'That's a bit of a jump.'

'We'll see, Hope, but if it's drugs, they won't be too shy about disposing of any officers on the right track.'

'He'll be fine, Seoras. You worry too much.'

'I pray to God that you're right, Hope, I really do. But I don't get feelings like this lightly.'

Chapter 10

Ross opened his eyes, aware that he could not remember them closing. The ceiling above him was high and his back hurt. He could feel he was still in his work clothes and the fluff of a blanket was tickling his nose. The ceiling above was barely lit by a light coming from some distance away. Oh hell, he was on a case and—

Ross sat bolt upright and started to look around him. There were screens at the far end of the hall. That was where Lucy had formed her makeshift morgue and forensic laboratory. And Kiera Harris was here, somewhere. Flicking his head around he saw Sergeant Sutherland walking towards him with a steaming cup of something.

'You're awake, Ross, good man. Here's something to get you going. Don't worry, you've only been asleep an hour. I didn't want to wake you as you hadn't had any kip since we started.'

'Anything happen while I was out?'

'Don't be so melodramatic. Nothing. I took a walk up to the fire and it's all but out. There are embers but they are going nowhere. It's safe but too hot to walk around. I was thinking Lucy should be heading that way soon though.'

'And how is our patient?' asked Ross, taking the mug in his

hands and sipping at the scalding liquid inside.

'Hasn't woken up. But she's been breathing normally as far as I can tell. Lucy checked her over but she's not the most forthcoming with her ideas. In fact, I think she reckons she's a bit classier than me. Just blanks me if I say anything.' Ross watched the man shake his head and he understood the feeling. Ross knew Lucy's story and still found her awkward to deal with.

'She's on the spectrum, as they say, Sergeant. It's nothing personal, just the way she is but it does feel like a cold shoulder. But if she's let the girl lie there then that's the best thing for her. I think we should get Orla back up to her house and to bed. She's had quite a shock and Kiera's going nowhere.'

'Are you still intending on bringing the communications back online? There's been nothing yet. I was wondering on how you reckoned on getting them re-established.' The Sergeant's face was grim and Ross thought he saw a touch of fear in his eyes. Fear was not a bad thing, keeps the mind sharp in some ways but it could turn into panic. Tom Sutherland had lost it before at the fire and Ross did not want a repeat performance.

'I'll go see the mayor and get him to take me round the communications and explain what's up. I also need to visit the Arnolds on the middle island. The family have several males and that body could be one of them. Also, Hamish MacArthur on the far island needs checked. I'll need to check the tides.'

'Shall I come with you, Ross?'

'Better if you stay put and guard Lucy and the evidence. I'll take the constable if you're in agreement, Tom. I'll just finish this cuppa and then I'll make a start and get Orla back to her house. I'll check back before going over to the other islands.'

Sergeant Sutherland nodded and made his way over to Constable Allen, briefing him on the day ahead. Ross stood up and then sought out the toilet facilities in the hall. There was only one toilet and the single hand basin had only cold water flowing. Gingerly, he cupped his hands and filled them before splashing his face. Several times he did this and began to rub his skin, attempting to put some life back into his features.

When he exited the toilet, he saw Orla McIlroy making daggers at Sergeant Sutherland who was trying to calm her down.

'Problem?' asked Ross.

'Miss McIlroy is refusing to go back to the house. Says she wants to be here when Kiera wakes up. Can't leave her partner.'

Ross stepped in front of the Sergeant and advised he would take it from here. 'Miss McIlroy, I'm afraid I need you to leave. There has been no indication that Kiera is going to wake up and my team will need to move out. I cannot leave a small team with you here. It's a matter of safety.'

'How the hell's it a matter of safety, Inspector? Are you wise? That's my Kiera there. I need to be here.'

'No, you don't,' said Ross giving his most compassionate face as he said it. 'What you need is sleep and to lock yourself away in your house until we get this all sorted. If Kiera awakens, we'll get someone to bring you straight here. And if she's fit enough, we'll bring her to the house to recuperate. But right now, I need you to go home. My apologies if that sounds harsh but these are the practicalities of the situation.'

'What harm does it do you having me sitting?'

'We have two dead and one person seriously injured. Until I understand what's happening, I want a curfew in this place. And that for you means in your house! Don't argue, Miss

McIlroy. It's for everyone's safety.'

'You think this was deliberate?' Orla's face showed shock, but Ross was not convinced. There would be resentment, a wish to find out who. Instead, the woman simply stood there as if she did not know what her next line should be.

'I don't know what to think yet. But I will. So, go home and let me find out.' It was classic Macleod, shutting someone down in firm but polite fashion and Ross had learnt that tougher side from the Inspector. Always a friendly man, Ross had known he needed a darker side, or at least a caricature he could play. 'I'm going in five minutes. Say your goodbyes as it might be a wee while until you see Kiera again.'

It was ten minutes before Ross, Allen, and Orla McIlroy left the community hall for Orla's house and said nothing when the men dropped Orla at her door. Instead, she closed it behind her without looking back.

'Friendly,' said Allen.

'Worth watching,' said Ross, but then he could say that about anyone here. Next, he went over to Paul Kemp who was sitting in the snow beside the dying embers of the fire. There was still smoke coming off the ruins and Ross could still feel heat despite the snowstorm around him. It was not as strong as last night but it was still weather that made you lean into it.

'All okay, Mr Kemp?'

'Yes, Detective. The fire's out. I'm more watching it in case anyone comes and has a look. They'll burn themselves, and badly too.' He shouted over the wind and Ross had to lean close to hear. 'People don't realise how long heat stays after a fire. But it's fine, keeping me warm.'

As Ross listened, he saw Daniella march across the snow in a leopard skin dressing gown carrying a plastic box of some sort and a flask. Without talking to Ross, she dumped the box beside Paul Kemp, kissed him quickly and then placed the flask on his lap. As she walked quickly back to the house, Daniella shouted over her shoulder with her arms folded tight around her. 'Sorry, Detective, but I'm not chatting out here.'

'Will you stay and make sure the fire remains down and everyone keeps clear?' Ross asked Kemp and the man nodded. 'When it's safe, please advise us at the hall. Our forensic lead will want to have a good look.'

'I can help if you want, Detective, ex fireman and that.'

'Excellent, I'll advise her but it's her decision.' Ross had no intention of involving Paul Kemp more than he had to but if he could keep everyone amiable then someone might just drop their guard and he could see what was happening.

It took ten minutes of banging the front door of the mayor's house and Ross was starting to worry when the bright, young but shy face of Autumn Forester appeared. Her father was just stirring, she signed, but they could come in if they wanted. Ross looked at the girl standing before him in her dressing gown and normally would have refused, but it was bloody cold. How Paul Kemp was sitting there so cheerfully, Ross had no idea.

Dad will be down in about five minutes, signed the girl and showed both men into the living room where Ross was delighted to see a stove. The hall was adequately heated and was at least standard room temperature, but the look of a stove added a few more degrees surely.

Tea? indicated Autumn.

'Sure,' said Constable Allen and asked for two sugars. When Ross went to speak the girl beckoned him with her finger and left before he could say anything, disappearing through a door.

90

Ross followed and watched her skip about the kitchen pulling out teabags. Looking at them closely, Ross saw they were not normal tea bags, all comprised of fruit or herbs. Infusions not real tea. But the girl still threw two heaped spoonfuls of sugar into Allen's mug.

When Autumn had made Ross's tea, she stood before him as he took a sip. Her gown was open, and her nightwear could be seen beneath. Ross imagined the Inspector getting flustered, but Ross felt nothing, just a girl infatuated with the man of authority who had arrived. *She'd been disappointed*, he thought. As Ross went to turn away, the girl reached out with a hand and pulled him close.

How's Kiera? She signed

'She's not great but she's stable,' Ross mouthed back.

And Alan?

How does she know my name? I don't remember saying it in front of her. Surely not. And then he thought to himself. *What are the rest of the islanders called?* 'Which one is Alan?' mouthed Ross.

The boy you pulled from the fire. You took him away. I was wondering if he was okay. Can you tell me? The girl was showing puppy dog eyes to Ross and he wondered just what she was feeling towards him. Was it an attempt to gain information or did she really have some sort of crush on him?

'The boy from the fire is dead, Autumn. I'm sorry. We haven't been able to identify him either. What makes you think it's Alan?'

There were tears forming in the girl's eyes and Ross thought for a moment he should hold her and give some comfort. But it would be inappropriate, even if needed, and her father could do that soon enough.

Alan and Kiera were, you know? Getting it together.

'How did you know?'

I saw them together, sneaking about the island. When the others were not looking, they held hands. Proper hand holding. He also held her by the beach. I saw them kissing. Not the basic stuff either. There were tongues.

Ross was bemused by Autumn's choice of words and he wondered how sheltered her life had been. But that was not the important issue. 'But did you see him enter the house with Kiera? Orla said Kiera ran into the house after it was ablaze.'

I don't know, I was asleep then. But don't tell father I said anything. He said not to annoy you.

Ross heard footsteps from the staircase near the front door. 'Okay, Autumn, our secret.'

Returning with Autumn to the living room, Ross saw Forester in his dressing gown and handed Allen his cup of heavily sugared fruit infusion. After the first sip, Ross saw the man nearly spit out the liquid.

'Mr Forester, we need to have a look at the communications systems you have here and see if we can get them back up and running. Kiera Harris is not in a good way and needs evacuated off the island. My officer has her comfortable, but she can't treat the damage caused by the fire.'

'You want to go out to sort it out in that? Can't it wait until this storm blows through?' The mayor cut a dishevelled figure in his faded dressing gown. Beneath it, Ross could see bare white legs and he thought the man was giving off the stench of stale alcohol.

'I don't want to, sir, but it is necessary. Kindly go back upstairs and get dressed for me. I'm sure your daughter will make you a quick breakfast if needed. Now, please, go on and get changed.'

Ross watched the man slowly turn back around and exit the room. Walking over to the stove, Ross stood with his hands out and tried to warm up. The lack of sleep was surely not helping how chilled he felt but there was no use focusing on that. Instead, he wondered what his colleagues back on the mainland would do. Surely Macleod would be looking to come over as soon as possible given the concerns he had raised about the death of Amanda Novak. When would this blasted storm cease?

It was fifteen minutes later when Ross struck out into the snow with Mayor Forester and Constable Allen. Almost immediately, he regretted taking anything to drink at the house as his bladder began to shout at him. But he ignored its screams as he pulled his coat up tight around him and fought through the snow behind the mayor.

The communications hut, room, or whatever it was, was located at the far end of the island. Walking close to the mayor, Ross heard him explain how everywhere on the island would have little towns, settlements of maybe six or seven houses growing into a vibrant community of maybe a hundred. At least that was the long-term plan. The other islands would be used for food production in fancy greenhouses. There would be some animal housing on Ceann Iar and fishing would be operated from Shivinish.

The dream of a larger settlement seemed wildly optimistic to Ross as he plunged his boots into inches of snow, but it did at least explain why they had to walk almost two kilometres to the malfunctioning communications systems. The path they struck seemed to cover the middle of the island and in the falling snow Ross struggled to see the crashing waves he could hear. How was the tide? Would he be able to cross to the other islands later?

The arrival at the communication system was a dreadful anti-climax. Ross had expected some grand sign, maybe lights that showed the entrance to the facility. But the building that housed the communications was simply a grey brick block. The mayor walked straight to the metal door at the front and pulled it open, ushering the police officers inside.

At first Ross could see little except some dull racking bathed in a dim green light. But then with a flick of a switch the room was bathed in light but to no better a sight. There were plenty of racks of equipment, but they all seemed to be dark.

'Shouldn't there be power to the equipment, Forester?' asked Ross, shivering. 'I understand the communications might be down but surely with the lights on there would be power?'

'I'll check the fuse box, maybe the main switch has blown or something.' With that Forester walked behind the main line of racking and opened up a box on the wall. 'Nothing's tripped on the box, everything is where it should be, all switched on.'

'So, we have lights but no power to the equipment,' mused Allen. 'Does the power split after the box for the lights?'

'I don't know,' muttered the mayor, throwing his hands up to the air. 'Alfie's the man for this. Well, at least he understands it better than me.'

'Do you understand electrics, John?' Ross asked his colleague.

'A little. I'll take a look.'

Ross watched Constable Allen make his way to the fuse box and then follow lines out of it along the walls. The man kept looking here and there around various pieces of equipment and shaking his head.

'Ross, you'd better take a look at this. Every bit of it's been wrecked.'

'Wrecked? What do you mean by wrecked?'

'Come round the back of the racking, Ross,' said John Allen, 'and you'll soon see.'

Stepping round to Allen, Ross understood what the man meant. There were wires everywhere, cut and splayed, stripped back to copper in places and others chopped in several places. Every item cut. Ross glanced at Mayor Forester who simply slumped to the ground.

'This changes things, Allen. Someone's deliberately trapped us here, deliberately cut off the communications. But why?'

The mayor was beginning to sweat now and started to gibber. 'One of our own, someone here. Autumn, I need to get back to Autumn. She's on her own in the house. Why did you make me leave her, Ross? You idiot, you've killed her.'

'Calm down, Forester, no one's dead. Why would anyone want to kill your daughter? You're not making sense.'

'You killed her! I tell you, she's dead.'

Ross motioned for Allen to step back round to the front of the racking with him and left the distraught mayor on the floor still shouting about his daughter. 'John, can any of this be fixed?'

'Doesn't look like it. At least not quickly. And you'd need a better craftsman than me. I was never an electrician, just assisted my brother with running wires and that. But this place is a mess.'

'Okay, what's your thoughts?'

'Without any weather forecast, Ross, all we know is that they thought this storm was going to last a few days. How bad it remains and whether anything can get here is unknown. But Kiera Harris needs medical attention. If there's a boat with a radio on one of the other islands, then maybe we should go for that.'

'I'm with you on that. But why do this? Who knows what? We're effectively closed in, a cage made by the storm and the sea. But what I don't understand is why we were called here in the first place?' Now Ross dropped his voice to a whisper. 'If someone wanted Amanda Novak out of the way, then why not simply throw her off a cliff into the sea after killing her. Lucy says she was murdered but why dispose of the body as a suicide with such marks remaining. Unless they weren't counting on Tom's intuition. His thoroughness in checking the body may have caused this. But what's so special that people need silencing? It's just an eco-community.'

'I don't know,' replied Allen, 'but we need to stay together until the cavalry arrives.'

'You're assuming it's going to get here in time.'

Chapter 11

Kirsten Stewart hated driving in the snow. She had set off at four in the morning to avoid traffic but on hearing the A9 had closed its more mountainous stretch near Aviemore, she had taken the road over to Aberdeen on the east coast before driving south to reach Dundee. With the conditions, it had taken four hours without a break and the city was coming alive as she entered the centre.

Parking in a multi-story, Kirsten first sought out a coffee house to grab some breakfast. Her stomach rumbled and she knew a cuppa might perk her up. Kirsten pulled a beanie onto her head, and then zipped up her fleece before making her way down the concrete steps of the car park and out into the Dundee air. After stopping for twenty minutes to eat a hot bacon roll and drink some thick and rather disgusting coffee, she followed the mapping on her mobile and reached the entrance to the Regency Hotel. The building loomed over her and she could see at least eight stories. Whilst not high for somewhere like London, this was an impressive monster in Dundee.

As she walked up the steps, a doorman, complete in uniform, eyed her suspiciously before intercepting her when he was sure she wanted to enter the building.

'Can I help you, madam?'

'You can open the door, thank you.'

'I'm afraid you'll need to state your business.'

Kirsten stopped and glowered at the man from behind her glasses. Her diminutive form and rather casual dress sense often provoked this unfair reaction and she relished producing her credentials and telling the man to hurry up and open the door.

'Of course, officer, but what is your business?'

'My own is what it is. If I need your help, I'll summon you. Now aside.'

Removing her beanie when inside, Kirsten made her way to the reception where a smartly dressed young man beamed at her as she approached. As she stepped forward she watched him take in her complete figure, but he was looking at the clothing more than her shape.

'Can I help you, madam?'

'Yes, you can. I need to speak to the manager, pronto.' Kirsten again waved her credentials. 'And I mean now, sir.'

With that she turned her back but was satisfied when she heard the receptionist pick up a telephone and ask for Mr Dawson. While she waited, she marvelled at the grand entrance hall. The hotel was owned by a chain who had invested in the legacy the previous owners had established. As Kirsten remembered there had been a sell-out due to dwindling funds. But as an ongoing concern, the hotel was reported to be stable.

'Officer, I believe you requested to see me.' Kirsten turned round and a tall, lanky man with tiny round glasses looked at her intently. He wore pinstripe trousers and a jacket and waistcoat, and looked remarkably alert for the time of the morning. Certainly more alert than Kirsten felt.

'Thank you for your speedy arrival, sir. Can we go somewhere more private? What I have to ask should not be for public consumption.'

The man never blinked but instead politely asked Kirsten to follow him and led the way past the reception desk down a narrow corridor and into a brightly lit office. The desk that occupied the room was twice the size of Macleod's at the station and before it was a small coffee table and two facing sofas on either side.

'Miss Addair, tea for two, please,' said the man to the air in general and then to Kirsten, 'I take it tea is fine by you. Very vulgar to start a conversation with coffee at this time.' The man did not wait for an answer but instead sat down on the edge of a sofa and offered the opposite one to Kirsten. Opening her jacket, she sat down and observed the man who politely smiled until the tea arrived a minute later.

Miss Addair wore a tight skirt, but it ran past the knee and her blouse looked extremely formal. She carried the tea on a silver tray and placed it on the table before Stewart and Mr Dawson. As the woman turned to leave, Mr Dawson coughed gently.

'Miss Addair, if you would be so kind to take a note of this meeting. I take it that's all right by you, officer. It is just that if this is formal business a note should be made for my employers.'

'By all means,' replied Stewart but she reckoned this was over the top. With Miss Addair installed with a pencil and pad, silence filled the room.

'I need to ask you about a stay at this hotel, Mr Dawson,

99

and about a guest. Her name was Amanda Novak and she stayed here for two nights on this date,' Kirsten pushed a piece of paper at Mr Dawson, 'with a gentleman who paid for the room. I believe his name is Mr Bonnar.'

At the mention of the name, Mr Dawson's eyebrows were raised and he turned to Miss Addair dismissing her. The man waited until his secretary had left the room before turning back to Stewart. 'The man you mention is a rather private individual. May I ask what your concern is about this particular stay?'

Kirsten stood up and for once felt on a level with the man. At his height, he was well over six foot. Now on her feet Kirsten felt she could make direct eye contact without appearing to stare up a mountain.

'The body of the young woman has been found in suspicious circumstances and I am following up her movements and contacts. As such this enquiry is routine but may lead to further investigations. I note that you sent Miss Addair away which tells me that this particular client of yours is a regular and important business to you. I appreciate that, Mr Dawson, but I am investigating a death, so please do not hold back any relevant details which could be inferred as your obstructing the police.'

The man coughed as if insulted by Kirsten's tone before smiling again and taking the teapot. 'Never the milk before, don't you think? Please sit down, officer, and we shall be civil about this. Of course, I will not hold back any details. Sugar?'

Kirsten shook her head and sat down opposite the man again and automatically felt small again. Taking her tea, she sipped it and found it to be warm if a little too bitter for her but there was no way she would let the man opposite know anything was wrong.

'Mr Bonnar is not a customer, officer. Pardon me, I never asked your name.'

'DC Stewart, sir.'

'Well DC Stewart, Mr Bonnar is a silent owner of this hotel. You will never see him around here except when he stays over. But he is the guiding and financial power behind this hotel although it is in his estranged wife's name. Now I am at liberty to advise you that since he became a single man again, he does invite new partners, in the relationship sense of course, for a weekend in Dundee. He's very proud of this town, particularly enjoys the V&A museum, and the Discovery, of course. Captain Scott is a particular inspiration to him, he told me.' The man narrowed his eyes. 'But understand it is all legal, consensual, and above board. If this young lady were with Mr Bonnar, she would have been a guest and treated with civility by Mr Bonnar and his staff.'

'Where does he stay in the hotel?' asked Stewart.

'On the top floor, in the suite reserved for him.'

'And does he occupy it often.'

Mr Dawson smiled politely but Stewart could see the man's annoyance growing. 'He does not advise me of his calendar until the last minute but on average I'd say he spends about a month a year here, in blocks of two to three days at a time.'

'May I see the suite upstairs?'

Mr Dawson seemed thoughtful. 'One moment, I shall ask Mr Bonnar's permission.' With that the man exited the room quickly.

Kirsten was left with an elegant tea set and some rather dainty biscuits before her and she snaffled half of the plate by the time Mr Dawson returned. 'Ah, I see you are rather peckish. I must advise you that Mr Bonnar has agreed to you

101

seeing his suite but that he requests that I accompany you. He also asks that you replace everything as it was.'

'Very good of Mr Bonnar. Please lead the way, sir. I'll be right behind you.' Kirsten watched the man sniff and turn away and quickly pocketed more of the dainty biscuits.

The suite was magnificent. There were elegant pictures on the walls, some sculptures sat on pedestals, and an elegant array of furniture in the main living area. Overall, there were five rooms: the main living room, complete with a giant television and a stocked bar. There was a master bedroom with a king-sized bed, resplendent in a blue and yellow duvet which somehow managed not to appear gaudy. An en suite to the bedroom featured the most luxurious shower Kirsten had ever seen and was only outdone by the bathroom with its whirlpool. The last room was an office with a solid oak desk and a large bank of computers.

'How many times did Miss Novak come here, Mr Dawson?'

'Just the once. My employer has a number of such retreats. I'm not sure Miss Novak fully appreciated Dundee. A woman of more foreign tastes.'

'Such as Milan, Barcelona or maybe the Baltics?'

'I believe Ibiza was more her thing, officer. Is there anything else?'

Kirsten swept her eyes across the suite but there was really nothing to look at in terms of the investigation. After all, the place would have been cleaned and all traces removed of Miss Novak, or at least anything incriminating.

'Just one thing, Mr Dawson, that you may be able to help me with. Does Mr Bonnar have any dealings with Viscount Donoghue?'

'Professional or personal?'

'Either.'

The man seemed to think for a moment, maybe sizing up just what he should say. 'The Viscount is a major player in Mr Bonnar's business dealings. A rival, not a partner. As such there have been business hostilities and Mr Bonnar considers that the Viscount has on occasion operated outside the laws of fair play. So, I would say the atmosphere between the two men is somewhat cold.'

Kirsten nodded and allowed herself to be directed to the lift. Inside she thought about the suite again and wondered what it would be like to stay there for a weekend, maybe even with her brother who would adore that large television. 'Mr Dawson, how much does a suite like that cost to stay in?'

'Well, that suite is not for hire as it's Mr Bonnar's personal dwelling. But we have a similar suite on the floor below and I doubt your senior officer, Detective Inspector Macleod would be able to afford a weekend stay.'

'I think he does all right.'

The man coughed again, and Kirsten awaited the patronising comment. 'With respect, he could not afford it if he committed his entire salary for the year to it.'

That was probably a somewhat wild statement, thought Kirsten, but she recognised that a marker had been thrown down. She never said who she worked for or even what division she had come from. But Dawson knew who she was. Kirsten had never been threatened so civilly in her life.

Kirsten returned to the car park where she scoffed the secreted biscuits and then drove out of Dundee towards Perth. Her investigations into Viscount Donoghue had shown he had an estate near Birnam, north of Perth and she hoped after visiting it, she could catch a now cleared A9 back up to Inverness. That was unless her boss had other need of her. Kirsten took the back roads towards Coupar Angus before turning west and heading for Birnam. As she drove the Old Military Road west, Kirsten noted that the road was clear except for a black car that was racing up behind her.

The vehicle was certainly breaking the speed limit and Stewart prepared herself to put on the car's hidden lights and bring the miscreant to a stop. As the black vehicle raced by, Kirsten sounded her siren and drove after the miscreant. There was no chase. Instead, the black vehicle, which she now reckoned was a Porsche, came to a halt, pulling off into a lane that was at the near side of the road. Kirsten perceived this as strange. Normally boy racers would show off a bit before stopping.

Parking her car behind the vehicle, Kirsten started a dashcam before stepping out of the vehicle. The air was cold and her breath went ahead of her. In the wing mirror of the Porsche, Kirsten saw a man, maybe fifty years of age, dressed in a sharp tie and shirt. Cautiously, she knocked the passenger window. It rolled down.

'Apologies, DC Stewart, but I needed to grab your attention. Would you kindly join me in the car?'

'Mr Bonnar, I presume.' Kirsten lent on the edge of the window and stared at the man inside. He was sombre looking but had a face weary with lines. 'My mother told me never to get into a car with strange men, and my boss frankly forbids it. Maybe you could step out and we can talk across your bonnet.'

'They said you can handle yourself, a mixed martial artist. And a wise move asking me to step out. I'm probably stronger than you and in a confined space could best you. But out there, I will be at a gross disadvantage. In light of your charms and my rude method of grabbing your attention, I will submit to your wishes.'

Mr Bonnar stepped out of the car and faced Kirsten across the black bonnet of the Porsche. He was at least six feet four and maybe more. His neck was thick with muscle, and his shoulders looked powerful. Kirsten reckoned his assertion that he would be at a disadvantage was incorrect. She pushed her glasses up her nose and concentrated, the fatigue of the early start making her muscles feel lax and weary.

'You have my attention, Mr Bonnar, so please how can I help you aside from advising you to slow down on your travels?'

'You were asking after Amanda Novak, and I wanted to get the record straight. I know she's dead. Someone on that accursed island did it but they would be following orders. The real culprit is in Amanda's recent past. Don't get in the way of me finding out who it is.'

The last words came with a sneer. 'Recent past? I agree with you, Mr Bonnar, and hence why I was visiting your hotel. Amanda stayed there with you. Is Mr Dawson correct in his tale of loving bliss between Amanda and yourself. I assume that's your tale as Mr Dawson probably follows instructions to the letter?'

'Indeed, he does. I'm not who you want, DC Stewart, but you won't find the person either. At least not before someone does and justice is meted out.'

'That's our role, not yours. When did you last see Amanda?' Stewart now walked around the bonnet. The key thing about those who wanted to boss a situation was to make sure you did the opposite of what they wanted. At a distance, the man had a diffuser, the car bonnet, if Stewart upset him. He would not want to openly kill an officer, if that was the type of thug he was. Too easy to be caught out by passing traffic.

And then something caught Stewart off guard. The man actually cried. His tears flowed and while he stood tall, he was clearly in pain.

'It was that weekend. We haven't touched the suite since then. She left me, after a year of fun and frolics. Said there was a new start, someone else. And then she went to that island. I had no contact, no farewell. So, don't get in the way, officer. There are debts to pay.'

'Who is it? Who stole her?'

But the man had climbed back into his car. Stewart's car was blocking the exit to the road, but the Porsche started and drove off in a blur down the rack they had joined from the main road. Stewart stood watching it go and then calmly pushed her glasses back up her nose and got into her car. It was too cold to stand around thinking outside. As she started her own engine, she thought what it must be like to be wined, dined, and then put up in a suite like The Regency had. Neat car too. It would be fun but if she ever got the chance her blasted conscience would soon call a halt to her festivities. What it must be to be carefree. Carefree and dead.

Chapter 12

Hope had breakfasted at six, spending a half hour with Macleod before they went their separate ways. To her, Seoras was looking tired, worried, and he rarely was that without being accurate to some degree about what was bothering him. He was also splitting his team wide which was not normal. Sure, he followed different lines of enquiry, but rarely would he not have them in pairs. And he was heading for Ross, so that was where he perceived the greatest danger.

There were still no communications with the Monach Isles, and she had heard Macleod field calls from the senior uniformed officers about their own colleagues stuck on the island. Time was of the essence and so Hope decided to look for some answers in Amanda Novak's past. It would be a long shot but maybe something would come up. The woman had travelled to far-off places but surely, she must have had some friends, a girlfriend to tag along with or maybe a male counterpart. Hope thought she knew the type of woman Amanda was, but you could never really tell. It was all a bit of guesswork and then taking your wins when they came and making the most of them.

The wind had not relented and Hope faced the day in her boots and leather jacket. It was the long one, reaching to her thighs and not the short jacket she wore in summer. A cream jumper sat underneath, and she was glad of its warmth as the icy wind blew across her face on the way to pick up the car. First stop would be Derek Novak, see if he remembered any of Amanda's old friends and then she would seek out any possible contacts from the paperwork at the house. She would be at Derek's house in twenty minutes and the hour was ridiculous to be calling for information, but Macleod's manner played on her mind.

Hope always thought she looked her worst when she rolled out of bed in the morning and for Derek Novak, the same was true. The whisky from the previous night was still on his breath and he burped loudly as he answered the door. Staring at Hope, he looked somewhat bemused.

'I thought you got everything last night?'

'We only got started last night, Mr Novak, and apologies for the early hour. I was wondering if you had any contacts of Amanda's in your phone book. Email addresses, numbers, whatever.'

The man swayed and Hope made to catch him, but he righted himself and then turned back into his hallway. Following the man, Hope watched him flop into a settee that had the stains of a pizza from the previous night. In fact, Hope wondered if any managed to get into his mouth at all.

'I don't even remember ordering that,' Derek said on seeing her look.

'It's not important. Contacts, Derek, where are the contacts?'

'Yeah, okay. See the table across from me, the one with the lamp on it?'

'Yes.'

'Well, not that one. Go to the right and—no, actually left go left, sorry getting confused. That's it. Open it. And the wee book, bring it here.'

Hope, having followed the instructions, found a little black book, and almost laughed at it. She didn't actually think people kept stuff like this. 'Many girls in this, Mr Novak?'

'Alas, Detective, no. I know what it looks like, but it is literally my address book. I wish it weren't.'

'But you knew some of Amanda's friends then.' Hope crossed the room and put the book into Derek's hands.'

'One, but she was her best friend. And we don't talk now. Not after the misunderstanding. Thought she liked me; I really did.'

'I don't need to know details,' said Hope, 'but I do need the number. Can you show me?'

Derek flipped the pages and then halted on the letter S. Hope leaned over as he traced his finger along various numbers before settling on a single word, Samantha. With that, he turned the book around so Hope was no longer reading upside down. 'I think you had better call,' said Derek. 'She'll hang up on me.'

Nodding, Hope took the book and stepped out of the room. With her mobile, she called the number in the book and got a disgruntled man on the telephone.

'Hello, hello?'

'Sir, It's DS McGrath from the Inverness police. I'm looking to speak to Samantha.'

The mobile was dropped and Hope could hear voices in the background beginning to argue. The man who had answered was swearing at someone who was rather calm. The voice sounded like a woman and stated that she couldn't care less but if the man would leave the money, that would be all. When the man became indignant, the woman advised that she would go to the man's house and speak to his wife. There was a lot of swearing but then Hope reckoned money had been left and a door slammed. Then the call was closed.

Hope rang again. The call rang for a minute and Hope wondered why an answer machine had not kicked in. And then a voice said, 'Hello.'

'This is DS McGrath looking to speak to Samantha, about her friend, Amanda.'

'Mandy? What about Mandy?' Hope could hear the tension in the woman's voice.

'I'm afraid she's died, ma'am. Am I speaking to Samantha?'

There was a pause and Hope heard sobbing before a blurted, 'Yes,' came back.

'I know this is hard, but could I speak to you about Mandy as I'm afraid her death was suspicious? Do you have somewhere we could meet?'

'You can come here if you want. I'm in Greenock, near the river. There's a number of us girls here so make sure you buzz the right flat.' The woman passed an address to Hope and the Sergeant thanked here and advised she'd be there in a half hour. It was a start.

Thanking Derek for his help and telling him to sleep off the booze and drink plenty of water, Hope took the car towards Port Glasgow and then on to Greenock. The address was in a back street and the area looked extremely downtrodden. A few of the windows in the street were boarded up and Hope made sure to lock the car. Arriving at a semi-detached clothed in that grey plaster that keeps the weather out but looks like a beaten-up raincoat at the same time, Hope found a buzzer at the door with four different names. She pressed for Samantha.

The door opened after a minute and Hope looked at a young woman dressed in a black silk gown which appeared slightly see through. Underneath she wore a jumper and some colourful leggings. Invited in with the wave of a hand, Hope followed the woman up the stairs and to a room. The air was cold but once she entered the bedroom, she found it was sweltering. An air heater bellowed in the corner.

'Costs a packet,' said Samantha following Hope's eyes, 'but the men like it. Makes you sweat. Until they get a headache.' The woman laughed at this and sat down on the bed offering Hope a seat at a small desk. On the desk were a number of play items and Hope tried not to shake her head. She'd never needed any of that stuff to make relationships fun. But then again, she doubted many relationships occurred here. It was the lack of relationship that kept this industry going.

'Is it true? Mandy's dead?'

'I'm sorry. She died yesterday morning, in suspicious circumstances. But she seems to be a rather private woman which is why I need to work out who her circle was and what she was doing on the Monach Isles.' Hope watched the woman's face and it held steady for a moment but then she shook her head.

'If she's dead, what the hell does it matter? But it didn't come from me, you understand. Some of the people Mandy kept company with were rough.'

'And you don't sound like someone who can't handle rough from the call this morning.'

Samantha raised an eyebrow. 'You heard all that. He wasn't rough, just a loudmouth. In this game you get that, and besides, he was embarrassed. Not a great performance.' There was a laugh and then she reached for a dresser drawer, taking out a packet of cigarettes. 'You smoke, love?' Hope shook her head. Samantha lit up and took a long drag of the stick in her mouth. Hope waited but the woman seemed like she was never going to speak.

'You were going to say about Mandy?'

'Oh shit, yeah. Sorry, was just thinking. Me and Mandy go way back, and we had some fun, you know. She played men; I mean really played them. I stroke their egos and for a price they get to enjoy me, but Mandy could actually reel them in so they believed they were something to her. It was her greatest asset, and her real trouble, too. With me, they look, enjoy, but there's another woman lining up to replace me. No emotional attachment, I make it a rule. You got to be cold in this business.

'Now Mandy left them thinking they had really got to her. Not a good thing and we had problems with guys arriving with flowers and then holidays. About three years ago, she asked me to come along to do a job with her for a real top-notch client. The man had money, real money. So, we did what we do, and he takes a real liking to our girl. He starts taking her away with him on holidays.

Hope reached for her mobile and brought up an image of the pictures they had found in Amanda Novak's house. 'Would these be from those trips?'

'That's the one. Don't get me wrong—the guy was really good to her, never lifted a finger. And she got money. But that was when she started doing the serious shit. Proper drugs. Normally we'd rarely take anything, maybe once in a blue moon if a client were insistent. But she formed a habit. And then someone else started feeding that habit. And I started losing touch with Mandy.'

Hope watched the woman begin to cry, tears running down her face. She sniffed them back and took another drag on the cigarette.

'Who was the new guy feeding the habit?'

'I don't know, not sure if it was even a guy. Maybe it was group of them, but I never got invited. And then she was off to that island. I'm off to an island in the sun is how she put it on the mobile. And then not long after she never answered the mobile. And then it stopped ringing.'

'Do you have that number?' asked Hope.

'Sure. I heard nothing else except from that guy she had been with. A couple of his thugs stopped me one night out there and gave me a grilling. I just said what I knew. They never touched me in the end, but I knew they would if I didn't say.'

'And who was the guy?' asked Hope.

'Bonnar. Although he had a pet name. But you are not getting that. He'll kill to keep that one quiet.'

Hope went to laugh but then saw the woman was not joking. There remained a silence and Hope thought Samantha cut a sad and lonely figure, genuinely grieving for her friend. Given her surroundings, the moment of compassion seemed surreal and became more so when the activities of a neighbour filled the air.

'And you don't know anything about this new group she was with—who gave her the drugs?'

'No. If Bonnar's men didn't get it from me, I don't know anything about them. Trust me. He would not have gone lightly on me.'

Hope heard something at the door. It was faint but as if someone had stumbled. It was the oddity of the noise

113

rather than its loudness and it had cut through the melodrama happening next door. Standing up, Hope indicated that Samantha should keep talking but the woman stopped and stared, watching Hope quietly slide across the carpet. And then there were heavy footsteps bolting down the stairs.

Hope opened the door and saw a black beanie with a mop of red hair swinging from under it as a figure exited the front door. Taking the stairs two at a time, Hope landed hard at the bottom, bouncing into the door frame but then managed to keep her momentum going as she fell out of the front door. Her target was now in the street and running along it at full pelt. Hope opened up her stride and followed as hard as she could. The road swung round the estate in a long curve and Hope believed she was gaining ground.

The redhaired listener looked around and seeing Hope closing, cut left into the driveway of a house. Hope jumped the wall at the front of the house, cutting the corner, and tore round the edge of the house. As she saw the driveway at the side of the house, she knew she'd been outthought. An arm was at head height and caught her under the throat, causing her legs to swing out from under her and she fell hard onto her back.

A fist came down at her, but Hope managed to roll aside, and she heard her attacker cry out, hitting her hand on the concrete. Breathing hard, Hope righted herself as the attacker turned to run. A desperate arm grabbed the attacker's leg and she fell in front of Hope who sprung forward onto her like a cat. A hand grabbed Hope's hair, pulling it hard but Hope dug her nails into the attacker's leg causing her to let go. Rolling clear, Hope stood up and closed off the attacker's exit back to the road as the rear door of the house opened. Two young men in boxer shorts and t-shirts stood looking at the duelling women before them.

'Wow, a real bitch fight!'

Students, bloody students, thought Hope. *They'll just stand there and watch, probably film it on their mobiles.* 'I'm DS McGrath and I'm apprehending this woman. Now either help or get out of the way.'

The first man stepped back but his friend strode out on to the driveway. 'I'll arrest her. Looks perfect to get tangled up with.' And he ran at the redheaded listener who promptly delivered a kick to between his legs, flooring the young man before he had even started.

But it was enough for Hope to get close and she grabbed her attacker's arm, forcing it behind her back and then drove her down to the ground with a foot placed at the rear of the knee. Within a few seconds, Hope had her handcuffs out and had subdued the woman. Hauling her back to her feet, Hope looked at the young man kneeling on the ground clutching his genitals.

'Thanks, are you okay?' The man's housemates had now appeared from the back door laughing loudly and the man tried to stand up, but he was in obvious pain.

'Ask her to rub it better,' said one of the new arrivals. Hope glowered at him.

'Another quip like that and I'll put you in these handcuffs, mister. You can get time for being lewd to an officer.' The man's face fell and while not strictly true, Hope's words had the desired effect. As she walked away, she heard one of the men saying she looked like that woman from the films, the superhero. Hope knew who they meant, and she desperately wanted to swagger like the woman from the film. Being professional was no fun sometimes.

As Hope returned to the house, Samantha came out to meet her, still in a dressing gown. Seeing that Hope was hot and sweating, and had another woman in tow, Samantha excused herself. Hope had what she needed from the woman and wanted to talk to this miscreant anyway, so placed the woman in the car, hands cuffed behind her.

'Name?'

'Helen Lilly, private investigator.'

'You registered as such or is this just a bit of freelancing.'

'I'm registered. You can check if you want.'

'Oh, I will but first I think we need to have a wee chat, because you have turned up twice now during my investigations. You also smacked my boss and that's not taken lightly. So, what's the deal? Who hired you; who are you chasing?'

'Okay, I've been employed by John Flaherty. His daughter's missing and has been for nearly two years after last being seen with a girl from the university. But I have no names. The last sighting I have of her is with Mandy Novak.'

'But Amanda Novak is on the Monach Isles, so what are you doing here?'

Helen smiled at Hope. 'I'm registered in Northern Ireland and have only been on this case for a week. I'm doing rather good to be here already.'

'What age are you?'

'Twenty-five.'

'Any experience in this field?' The woman shook her head. 'Well, first lesson, don't hit any police officers, instead own up and if your work's legitimate you might get told to piss off, but you'll not get arrested.'

Helen looked indignant. 'How was I to know you were

police? Everywhere I've gone there's been people investigating, and none of them have worn uniforms.'

'What people?'

'I don't know them all but some of them were working for a Mr Bonnar.'

Hope shook her head. 'Good job you bumped into me. You have no idea who you're getting involved with. I think you, me, and my boss need to have a proper chat about what you know.'

Chapter 13

Macleod was at a loss once Hope had departed. It was his fervent prayer that the weather would relent at least enough for a flight to Benbecula and from there, he would be able to somehow get over to the Monach Islands. But the snowstorm was relentless and he saw no aircraft depart. Surely if he could reach Benbecula, someone would be prepared to take him over the rough sea to Ceann Ear. It was only another fifteen kilometres.

Stuck in his hotel room, Macleod decided he needed to put the time to good use and first called his partner Jane. He had not had much time to speak the previous evening and now he made his apologies. Although she spoke back, he got the feeling she was pushing him off the call. There was this thing she had: if he was working then let him work. A few minutes later he was back at the window of the hotel looking at an incredibly quiet airport.

His mind wandered back to the characters on the island. His sudden announcement to Hope that the roll call looked like a team to make your own drugs was a bit of a wild response but the more that he thought about it, the more it seemed a possibility. After all, why else would all these people be there.

But if they had been a pilot, a stewardess, a holiday rep, a travel agent, and a man with two bats that were different colours on either side, would he have announced they were opening an airport?

And what about the others? There was a fisherman there. Amanda Novak: why was she there, ardent tourist and good time girl? And a family. Where would you make the drugs? Surely everyone would have to be in on it. He could not make it fit. Not entirely.

And Kiera Harris? Another one who did not fit. Caught in the brothel house, an unknown with not a lot of past on record. Someone you'd not pay much attention to. Someone . . . disposable.

Macleod reckoned his mind was running away from him and stood up and grabbed his coat. A brisk walk to the terminal to grab a paper would help. Not that he would read it but otherwise he'd look like some sad and lonely individual. With a paper, he'd be a man of purpose. Except there were papers downstairs in the hotel lobby so the hotel staff would know.

Maybe he should have gone with Hope, but he did not want to miss any opportunity to get to the islands. Tucking his collar up, Macleod stepped out onto the crunchy snow and made his way along scraped pavements to the airport terminal. He saw a line of taxis wondering what else to do with their day because no one was travelling. A lone cleaner walked behind one of those large cleaning machines that reminded him of *Star Wars*. A security guard walked past and Macleod subconsciously pretended he had a paper and purpose to be there.

Why not Kiera Harris? She would not be missed and if she were into the drugs habit would be a perfect test vehicle for anything they made. And if things did not go so well, then she could always conveniently drop off a cliff into the sea. It would be hard to search out there and when she was found who would be interested in what chemicals filled her body. No family would pursue the truth.

Macleod saw the airline desk, the one for the flights that went to Benbecula and a woman sitting behind it looking very bored. As he approached, she barely looked up, and then when he coughed, standing before her, she nearly jumped.

'Sorry, love, you scared me. What can I do for you?'

'I was trying to get to Benbecula. Are all the flights cancelled today?'

'Both of them, love. Have you not seen the weather?' The look on the woman's face made Macleod think he was mad, but he had to try.

'Is the airport actually shut?'

'No, but no one's flying. They have snow ploughs out at the moment but that's just to stop the build-up so we can get started again as soon as possible. But we'll just have to hold out until then.'

'Is there anywhere I could charter something?'

The woman shook her head. 'If it's a wedding you're off to, they'll still be married if you stay put and you'll not be dead.'

The word resonated with Macleod. Maybe he was just working on a worst-case scenario, but the word scared him. Was Ross okay? If drugs were involved, then who knew. No, he was just getting overexcited, a result of being stuck on his bottom.

'Is there anywhere to hire a charter aircraft, a small one. Maybe a helicopter?'

'Listen, I don't think that's a good idea but if you want to try, head down and along to the desks through that door. There's a helicopter company there who do charters and a fixed wing operation, but I doubt they will be up for it.'

Macleod nodded and thanked the woman who shook her head in disbelief at him as he walked in the direction she had stated. *Blast this weather. Why did I have to be on that stupid course, teaching us how to speak to each other. None of them want to call me Seoras, and I'm not calling the boss Diane. She can be the DCI, or boss if we have to. There's a reason for the titles, a reason for everyone having their place. It just keeps coming, more and more changes. The technological ones I can handle but this pandering nonsense. Still, I'd better make sure I show I'm in touch or it'll be another black mark for me. But does it matter? How long can I stay in this job? If it's not the constant barbarity I see, it's this tiptoeing nonsense.*

Macleod's mood was foul when he approached the desks of the charter aircraft companies. He looked about but no one was there. As he tried to look behind the desks and then open a door in the rear, a man coughed, and he turned to see a man in police uniform holding a rifle delicately to one side. Beyond him was a similarly attired woman.

'What are you doing, sir? This is an airport and you need to keep to the designated areas. That door is for staff members only. Can I see your boarding card? Or your airport identification if you work here?'

Macleod bit his tongue. He was about to lambast the man but then he realised he was in the wrong. His impatience was making him not think straight. 'Sorry, officer. I don't have a boarding card or ID, as I was trying to speak to someone from the charter companies about hiring a plane.'

'In this weather, sir? Identification, please.'

Macleod slowly placed his hand into his long coat and produced his police credentials. 'Sorry, but I was really out of line there. I just need to get over to Benbecula. I'll just head back to the coffee shop and take a wee breather, get myself together, and not panic you anymore.'

Sometimes in life you had to put your hands up and simply explain you had made an arse of it. With luck, the officers would just brush it off and have a laugh between them, so it would not filter up or down in the police food chain.

'DI Macleod. Recognise the name. Constable Frasier, sir. '

'I believe the *sir* is now out of date after the conference I attended yesterday but thank you all the same, Frasier. I hope I didn't bother you too much.'

'No, Inspector. No trouble at all. I doubt you'll see flights for the rest of the day. Maybe best to try tomorrow.'

'Maybe I will, Constable, maybe I will.' But something told Macleod that would be too late.

At the coffee shop, Macleod took out a notepad and pen and began to jot down how he would set up a drugs operation on a remote island. This was relatively easy. You simply needed power, a clean room, and equipment, different skills from chemist to courier. A boat was required to get off the island. But what struck him was the sheer genius of placing the facility there. It was an eco-community, so you could keep visitors at bay as you wanted to have a different lifestyle. Like a cult where you wanted your practices to be secret, all you had to do was place it behind gates. A rough patch of sea would help too. But that was the answer—a gated community.

And if no one could see in, you could test your drugs and see the results properly. Amanda was a sticking point but then maybe he did not have her profile correct. Kiera Harris was the druggie but maybe Amanda dabbled too. That was a theory, and he would need to prove it. If only he had contact with Ross, he could steer him, find out what he knew, make a proper assessment. He needed to be there.

Macleod had an idea and rang through to the Aeronautical Rescue Co-ordination Centre, who looked after the Coast-guard helicopters. He knew it was a long shot but maybe he would be able to persuade them to get over to the islands. From experience, he knew they had helicopters capable of flying in the most extreme weather, but he was aware he was not in much of an emergency. The only injured person was dead, and he had lost contact with his colleague who was on a self-sufficient island with plenty of food and shelter.

The call lasted five minutes, mainly because Macleod made it stretch out that long and had requested to speak to the Aeronautical controller, the senior in the room. The answer was a firm but polite no. And he could not fault their logic.

His coffee now going cold, Macleod called Kirsten Stewart, but her phone rang out to the answer machine. Leaving a request for an update, he made his way back over to the hotel. As he slipped his shoes off and lay down on his bed to think, his mobile rang.

'Macleod.'

'Seoras, it's Hope. I have someone you need to talk to. A private investigator, bit raw but has been employed to look into Amanda Novak. I think you might be interested in what she has to say.'

'Well, she'd better have bit less attitude than that Irish one, Smythe. Where do you want to meet?'

'I'll see you in twenty minutes, Seoras. Probably best in one of the hotel rooms.'

Chapter 14

Macleod waited in the airport coffee bar. Hope had suggested the room in the hotel for secrecy, but Macleod reckoned the airport was so quiet after the flights had been cancelled for today that they were in no danger. Besides, the coffee in the room was rubbish and he needed a decent cup to keep his nerves in check. Constant thoughts of what Ross was doing were running through his head. If Macleod had been fortunate enough to have children then maybe this is what that tension parents feel would be like, but he forced himself to see Ross as only a colleague. But this was a lie. He was not a cherished son, but he had become a friend.

Hope strode into the coffee bar with a red-headed girl in tow. The two together made Macleod think they were some sort of double act, or in team colours but he threw away this ridiculous fancy and focused on the features of the pasty woman who accompanied Hope.

'This is my boss, DI Macleod, and this, sir, is Helen Lilly, who has been following me this morning. After a brief scuffle, we have come to an understanding, and I thought we should all have a chat about what Miss Lilly is doing as I think she could be at risk with the people she's investigating.'

'Very good, McGrath.' Macleod realised they had simply slipped back into the old way of speaking and he reckoned this was because they had someone present. There was a degree of showing them the importance of your colleague and that they were in a formal setting. If Macleod had called McGrath Hope, then the tone would have been too friendly.

Helen Lilly sat down opposite Macleod and Hope penned her into the elongated bench, between herself and a window. *The woman looks nervous*, thought Macleod; *maybe it's her first time involved with the police.*

'Miss Lilly, where are you from?'

'Northern Ireland.'

Another Smythe, great. Patrick Smythe was a private investigator from Northern Ireland Macleod had run into several times. Although useful, Macleod found the connection not to his liking. 'Whereabouts?'

'Belfast, but the office is based in Lisburn.'

'Tell me how you got into this investigation of mine, right from the top. You've been entangled with one of my officers and in not a friendly way. I believe you also managed to lamp me with one the other night, so you really need to be showing us you're a friend and not an enemy at the moment.'

Helen hung her head and if she had not been so white to begin with, Macleod reckoned she would start to look like the Arctic. Her hands were before her on the table and were beginning to shake.

'I received a call from John Flaherty, about his daughter, Mary, who had been missing for over two years. She had previously gone to Glasgow and Mr Flaherty had maintained telephone contact, the weekly call and that. But then it all stopped.'

'Was there any reason?' asked Hope.

'No, nothing. The telephone calls from her simply ended. He dialled the number, and it was disconnected. So, he started calling any numbers he had previously. Nothing.'

'Did he come to the police?' interjected Macleod.

'No. Mr Flaherty is a man who does not trust the police. He is rather old, but his past was from a time when his side of the community and the police did not see eye to eye and well, Mr Flaherty did things they would say were very unlawful. He would say he was defending his country. I didn't go into too much detail. You don't back home. The man was missing a daughter and wanted her back. I tried to keep it that simple.'

Leaning forward, Macleod stared into Miss Lilly's eyes. 'I'm trying to decide if you are very stupid or very ignorant. Regardless of any political or sectarian bias, you get a character like that from any community and you make sure you understand their background and links. You wouldn't want to step on the toes of someone who would take a serious aversion to your presence.'

'I did do checks,' spurted Helen Lilly, rearing back from Macleod. 'He was out of favour with a lot of people; that's why he was using someone like me and not going through some old networks. "Things have changed", that's what he said. "No more good connections to put pressure on people as and when."'

'Sounds delightful,' said Hope, waving over a man behind the coffee counter.

'McGrath, hardly the time.'

'And you've been in a café all morning, sir, I'm chilled through. Miss Lilly?'

Macleod shook his head but waited for the man to take Hope's order. Maybe he had a different view of Helen Lilly to McGrath. Unlike Patrick Smythe, the other Irish Private Investigator Macleod had previously dealt, this woman was an unknown. Smythe had shown himself through previous encounters to be trustworthy and remarkably competent but Miss Lilly needed to be kept at a suspect's distance. Seeing the coffee arrive some four minutes later, Macleod gave Hope a look, indicating he would like to get on and Hope turned back to Helen Lilly.

'Why did you take the job?'

'Money. I did a little work for an uncle of mine and was setting up on my own. Work's been hard to get. There's been some wives and husbands checking up on each other, but this was the first real job of any merit. I couldn't not take it.'

'So, what did your investigations uncover?' asked Macleod now with an empty coffee cup and looking at McGrath for not ordering him one.

'Traced her from her old address to a rough part of Maryhill in Glasgow. She had been in a drug den there, but she had moved on. Apparently, she had done well for herself and was seeing another girl from Ireland but this one was from the south, Dublin, some said.'

'Got a name for her?' asked Hope.

'Just "Orla", that's all they said. I was looking for a photograph, but Orla never appeared in any. She was much classier, people said, but she was also a snob. Never wanted to be amongst Mary's friends, or at least the drug-addict ones. I'm not sure Mary had many others. That was until recently when I found a photograph of an older woman, maybe thirties. Mary and the woman were in a room together and it looked like some sort of interview or that as Mary was dressed much neater than any picture I had seen from her Glasgow time. The druggie who I got the picture from said they had stolen it because Mary was bragging about the big time and how she was going to be set up.'

'But how did you follow on from that? You had a nobody in a photograph.' Macleod looked quizzical.

'I asked around some known dealers who Mary had contact with. They were all very sheepish, said the woman was close to top connections or at least had been. You see Mr Bonnar had people around too looking into things. I managed to avoid them but it was nip and tuck a few times. He's quite a big deal to these people although they would not say much about him. I'm still not sure who he is but he's a main player. Still, I managed to get a name from one when he was high. Amanda Novak. It's not that common a name in the Glasgow area, so I went around checking up. And then you were investigating an Amanda Novak on my list. While you were at her parents, I was in the house, looking for anything that would indicate a new life. But I'm at a blank. She clearly travelled a lot and never seemed to pay.'

'And then you thought you would piggyback my Sergeant? Not a clever plan. You could have come to us.'

'My client would never have agreed to that, and given his background, that was not a risk I wanted to take. I'm taking a risk being here but you caught me so I thought I should explain my presence. And I know nothing about his criminal past, I made sure of that. At least nothing everybody doesn't already know.'

Macleod stood up. 'Not so daft after all, Miss Lilly. Wait there.'

Hope stood up and grabbed Macleod as he walked away. 'Where are you going?'

'To get a coffee, Hope. It seems this new friendlier level of team-working means my coffees no longer arrive.' Hope drew in a breath to speak but then saw Macleod's grin. It felt good to get a joke over her; it was usually him at the brunt.

As Macleod returned with his coffee, he could see that Helen Lilly had stood up and was at a table behind Hope. Raising his eyebrows, Macleod pointed to the private investigator.

'She's on a call, Seoras.'

'To whom?'

'Mr Flaherty. She did ask to take it and I thought it would be a good idea. She says he hardly ever rings her directly, instead taking reports through the mail. After all, it hasn't been the speediest investigation for her.'

'She looks worried, Hope. Bit of a face on her. This'll be interesting when she comes back. And by the way, how do we address each other to the public. I don't get using our first names in front of others when we are calling them by their second name. Too blasted confusing.'

Hope rolled her eyes. 'It was a whole day's conference. You were in a workshop. Just call me whatever, really. It's not like I'll be offended.'

Macleod nodded but deep down he was unconvinced. He had an ability to offend people, women especially and he was unsure where it came from. Maybe his upbringing in a place where women were always lesser. Sitting down, he drank his coffee, all the time watching Helen Lilly speak to her boss. Hope kept standing, at first because she would block Helen's access to her seat but then because she was also intrigued by the call. This was no regular update it seemed.

When Helen closed the call, she stood for a moment and aimlessly came back to the table and slid into her seat. Looking out the window, the woman seemed perplexed, bemused even. Macleod saw Hope go to speak but he held up a hand indicating she should wait. Whatever was troubling Helen Lilly, Macleod wanted a thoughtful answer, not some blurted and absent-minded offering. Slowly Helen returned to her drink.

'Trouble?' asked Macleod.

'That was Mr Flaherty. He's pulled me off the investigation.'

Macleod saw Hope's shocked face as she leaned forward. 'Why did he do that?' asked his partner.

'At first, he wouldn't give a reason. But when I pressed, he said that he had been formally asked to stop.'

'By whom?' Macleod found himself leaning forward as he asked.

'He wouldn't say. But I got the feeling it was not a request. Mr Flaherty for all his previous connections is a frail man and he has another daughter and grandchildren. I can only think they are under threat.'

'How was he?'

'How do you mean, Inspector?'

'Well, was he calm telling you all this? Was he looking for a way around it? Was he even satisfied? Try and get your thoughts about a job loss out of the way and ask how the man was. It might show you what's really happening.'

Helen Lilly stared back out of the window. 'Well, he was . . . ' The woman stared at Macleod. 'I was going to say, he was disappointed, anxious. But you're right. I'm anxious. This was good money; I also wanted a win so word would spread. But he was calm. Not like before. Inspector, he loves that girl. I know, he was so earnest before. I reckon he could kill to get her back. But now he's calm, like it's all been sorted. No, more like it will all be sorted.'

Macleod watched Hope's worried face but gave a quick flash of the eyes to let her know they would not be discussing the thoughts in her head in front of Helen Lilly. 'Miss Lilly, give me your phone number. And here's my card. Any developments, give me a call but as of now, stop working this case. It's a blow to you but this is not a man to go beyond his instructions. Go home, have a week off. But if anything of note comes up, please contact me. Do this and I'll forget what you've been up to. And not a word to Flaherty about what we have discussed. You can tell him you got lifted but only if he asks.'

Helen Lilly seemed to take it all in, but she still looked dumbstruck. With a nod of the head, Macleod instructed Hope to escort her out to a taxi. The woman's car was still back where Hope had caught her. With his table empty, Macleod put two hands around his coffee cup and stared into it.

He was in a strange situation, coming at a case from the wrong end. Usually, he was in the middle working the strands back to the start, finding a reason for what happened. But now he had the beginnings, all the pieces, and was trying to work out what had actually happened and not simply the reason. But with the information he had just heard, Macleod was now more worried for the safety of his people out on the island. Drugs had been mentioned again. And the people that dealt with drugs didn't give second chances. They would have no qualms about taking Ross or anyone else out of the game to cover things up. He needed to get onto those islands!

Chapter 15

Kirsten Stewart drove up the long and winding drive that led to the stone building with the small turrets. The estate of Viscount Donoghue was impressive and on presenting her credentials at the gate, she had been sent to the offices. It looked like no offices Stewart had been to before and when she tried to park her car, a man in a suit offered to do it for her. Gratefully acquiescing, Stewart entered by some large stone steps into a tartan-carpeted hall. A woman, in glasses that were probably more severe than even Stewart's, looked up briefly. Behind her was a shield with a number of swords protruding from it. A crest sat on the front of the shield.

Kirsten continued to stand and the woman looked up again over the top of her glasses. 'Can I help you?'

'Yes, ma'am, my name is DC Stewart, and I would like a word with Viscount Donoghue. I believe he was due to be on the estate today from an online diary I read.'

'Could I see some credentials?'

'Of course,' said Kirsten, pulling out her wallet containing her ID. 'Is the Viscount on the estate?'

'I'm afraid not, officer, as he has been delayed coming up

from London. In truth, all I had was a call from him to say he would not be returning today due to business concerns. I'm afraid it's a wasted journey.'

Stewart watched the woman return to her computer. 'Excuse me, ma'am, but would there be someone on the estate that has dealings with the Monach Islands who can give me a history of the Viscount and his company's involvement with the islands.'

'I'm sure we have a number of brochures on that subject. Let me see what I can find you.'

Stewart walked over to the desk and leaned on it. Due to her small stature the only thing visible to the woman was her glasses and the top of her head and it was not the impression Stewart had wanted. But she continued, 'This is a murder investigation, ma'am, and I need to speak to someone on this topic. If you can't find me someone then I will simply advise my boss, who will then be back within the hour with a whole host of people looking for answers and disrupting your day. His name's Macleod and he doesn't take any blocking attempt on his investigations lightly.'

'Well, then,' said the woman standing up abruptly as if to push Stewart backwards, 'I shall try and accommodate you, if you would be so good as to wait.' The woman offered a chair at the far wall but Stewart continued to stand.

'Absolutely, I'll wait.'

The receptionist was like a kettle who was fighting not to boil over, and Stewart stood within earshot of the phone conversation she then had. There were a few words of who is this woman but when Macleod's name was dropped it seemed that all hell had broken loose and Stewart distinctly heard the phrase, 'not that bloody bastard'. From time to time the woman would look at Stewart who kept a calm but smug grin on her face as she awaited someone to come.

After five minutes, a man appeared in grey jacket and trousers with some black, expensive-looking shoes. He stared first at Stewart and then at the receptionist. Clearly, he could not believe Stewart was the person he was to deal with for he waited for a nod from the receptionist before coming over to her. At six feet five and counting, the man dwarfed Stewart but she held that same grin.

'Hello, my name is Arthur Finchley and I represent the Viscount's interests here on the estate and in other parts of the United Kingdom. Mrs Green has advised that you need someone to talk to you about the Monach Islands and our rather daring community that's been set up. However, she says, rather alarmingly, that you are investigating a murder. As I understand it from communications we have received from the island, there has been a rather tragic suicide.'

Stewart looked up at the man, letting her glasses fall slightly so she was peering over the top. She had no need to, but it gave the look she wanted. 'I tend to find all suicides are tragic, sir. But this one is not just tragic; we have reason to believe it may be more than a suicide. And while I may have mis-phrased in saying a murder, do understand that we are treating the death as suspicious.'

The man rode the comment well and while not smiling, did not appear overly distressed. 'I believe you wish to talk to me about what we do on the island, is that correct?' The man did not wait for the answer but simply carried on. 'I'll be happy to furnish you with a little detail; after all, it was the Viscount's idea. He's quite a modern thinker but he's well aware that we all need to get back to a simpler way of life, Detective . . . oh, I am sorry. Mrs Green did say but your name seems to have slipped my mind.'

'Detective Constable Stewart, sir. Do you have items sent from here to the island? Or does anything come back here? Or is the island a fantasy that exists entirely on its own.' Stewart stared up at the man. *Forget her name, would he? Well, he was getting the works.*

'The island is entirely a design for life and has no monetary value to the Viscount. He sees it rather as his social duty to promote a lifestyle of simplicity and one that is in harmony with its surroundings.'

'But he's never felt the need to go there himself? I mean he doesn't have a shed of his own out there, braving the odd gale or that?'

The man gave a derogatory laugh and pointed towards the front door. 'Let me take you on a little tour of our storage facility for the island. There you'll see some of the more environmentally friendly practices we will be putting in so that the island can be its own source of fuel and power, and help the population fend for itself. This way, Detective.'

With that, the man strode out of the front door so fast that Stewart struggled to keep up. Outside, the snow was thick but the main road round the estate had been ploughed and Arthur Finchley led Stewart along without ever looking back. After a half-kilometre, he cut over to a large green barn and opened a small metal door in the side before asking Stewart to step through. Inside, lights came on automatically and Stewart saw an area lined with metal racking and a number of large wooden crates.

'And this is all part of the Viscount's dream, Detective. You see on the floor, crates that hold wave generators and wind turbines. Nothing too large—after all, we don't have that great a population out there. But even if we did, the wind turbines would be small and localised to each settlement.'

'Is that the end purpose, a lot more people on the island?'

'Not too many, I assure you, but we hope to have sustainable fishing, horticulture within domes designed for the wild conditions. I believe they have actually grown some peppers this year. And that's the point, to inspire others in places as remote and with as difficult a set of conditions but in other parts of the world. The Viscount is quite an inspiration.'

'I'll take your word for it,' replied Stewart, clearly not taking the man at his word. 'So, when does all of this get shipped out?'

'Over the next six months. Weather conditions can make it awkward and we are waiting on surveys from the people out there. There's a lot that goes into this. We are aiming to expand to another settlement within a year. But at the moment we are working out where it will be best to site the new settlement.'

'How do you convince people to go out there? I mean there's no real job. They must lose out on income and that.'

Arthur Green raised his nose to the air and Stewart reckoned he thought he was Winston Churchill speaking to the nation. 'We are pioneering the drive for a better lifestyle, Detective. Maybe someone such as yourself who deals with the darker side of the human psyche would struggle to comprehend or be inspired for such a mission.'

Stewart ignored the man and began to walk along the boxes and various items stored on the racks. 'Do you mind if I handle any of this?'

'Be my guest, Detective, there's little for you to damage. But some of it is quite heavy and I would suggest someone of your rather diminutive frame does not try to bite off more than she can chew.'

Stewart was ready to throttle the man. Arthur Green was a prime candidate for being Macleod's next case if he continued at this rate. But then she spotted a number of industrial fridges at the rear of the house. 'What's in those?'

'One of the benefits,' started Mr Green walking over to the fridges, 'of having a small fishing operation happening from the island is that we do get a supply of fresh fish that the Viscount enjoys, and which makes it to the various restaurants associated with his estate.'

'And it comes through here, first? I'd have thought you would be sending it straight to the restaurants and that.'

Mr Green snorted. 'It's a matter of logistics. I doubt you've ever had to handle any fresh animal product. It's all about timing.'

'Actually, my father was a fisherman.' Stewart grinned, hiding the fact that her father was not a fisherman and had actually been a postman. 'Do you mind if I take a look at the fish? A proper look?'

'Of course not,' said Arthur, but his sudden jolt of surprise at the question said there was more to the fridges than previously described.

Stewart delved into the freezer and lifted out a crate of fish. Carefully she picked fish after fish up, examining it and even smelling it. She had no idea if this was normal but then she reckoned Arthur had as little a clue as she did. By the time she was finished, Stewart had emptied about a fifth of the crates in one freezer. But she found nothing but fish inside and she stank.

'This is a sweet one, Mr Green. I haven't eaten yet. Any chance I could get one for my lunch?'

Green smiled broadly. 'Of course, I'll find you one that hasn't been labelled for its destination yet.'

As Green dove into another part of the freezer, Stewart removed one of the fish and placed it inside her jacket. When Green next looked back to her, she had placed the lid of the box back on and was stacking the boxes back into the freezer. After a quick tour of the rest of the items on the shelves and more about the ever-enterprising Viscount, Arthur came to an abrupt halt.

'I hope that has been useful to you?' asked Arthur but he did not seem to care. 'If there is any more information you need, then please do not hesitate to call me. I'll show you back to the main office if you don't mind. I have a meeting coming up shortly.'

Stewart followed the man back to the house but something was bugging her. Arthur Green had been a smug man for most of the tour but when she had asked to look at the fish, he had clearly become nervous. But she had found nothing. In fact, she had no idea if the fish were fresh at all. Her biggest problem was that she could not simply demand that all the fish be emptied. After all, a suspicious death had occurred but what link was there to the fish? Still, she had a sample, and not the one swinging in the plastic bag she was carrying.

Back in her car, Stewart drove clear of the estate by several miles and checked she was not being followed before taking the fish from her pocket and placing it in an evidence bag. She'd call the boss on the way back but right now she needed to drive back to the station and deliver a brace of fish to Jona Nakamura.

Chapter 16

As Ross reached the community hall, his feet were going numb and he welcomed the heat that swept out through the open door. Sergeant Tom Sutherland followed him through into the warm building and immediately sought out his colleague. Constable Allen, having opened the front door, was sitting across from a sleeping Lucy MacTaggart, and appeared rather glum.

'Chin up, Allen, we're back. Time to get a brew on.' Sutherland was relieved to be back inside and Ross reckoned it was because he felt safe here, locked inside the hall. Ross did not share the same belief and all he really wanted was to get off the island or have a large number of colleagues arrive to assist. With the power deliberately cut, the only option to contact anyone outside of the island was to make it to the Arnold's boat on the next island.

'Do they have any books or magazines around here?' asked Ross.

'Not bored, are you, Ross?' joked Sutherland, a little too readily. There was a madness behind the voice, Ross was sure, and the man, although holding it together now, could tip over if pushed.

'Wondering if they had any tide tables. I'm reluctant to walk through that snow and wind to find I can't cross to the other island. But we need to get a message, get some help for Kiera Harris. I take it she hasn't changed at all, Allen.'

'Lucy didn't mention anything and I didn't notice anything myself. She's just been sleeping. Lucy took to the bed about two hours ago. Poor girl's wrecked.'

'Then just let her sleep, Allen,' Ross advised as he delved into a collection of books he found at the corner of the room. 'And here it is, a tide table. There are some useful things here.' Ross flicked through the pages and then stopped suddenly with his finger tracing the table. 'And we are good to go in about an hour. Mind you, I wonder how long it stays okay to cross. We'll just have to take our chances.'

'Do you want me to come with you?' asked Allen. 'I mean the Sergeant has already done a trek.'

The Sergeant spoke up, 'No, you stay here, Allen; I'm good to go once I've had my tea. Best you bunker down here and wait for the re-enforcements to arrive. You're doing well, lad.'

Ross's ears picked up at the conversation and he walked up close to Sergeant Sutherland. 'How long has Allen been with you?'

'Two weeks. Transferred up from the Borders. Still learning the ropes.'

'Bit of a rough one, this then. But are you sure you don't want me to take him along instead? After all you've been out already, Tom.'

The Sergeant laughed, almost too much. 'No, best the kid stays here. He's not used to the storms we get.'

Ross was sure the Borders got a lot of snow and blizzards compared to the Western Isles, but he was not for arguing with a senior officer. Besides, he needed a quick drink and maybe some soup if he could find some before setting off. Yes, soup would be good. Part of Ross wondered how long Macleod or McGrath would wait before sending over more help. The conditions made it difficult and he guessed that they would not risk anyone without a definite indication of further trouble. They did not know though about the burnt-out house and the body lying in the temporary morgue beyond the screens.

It was another hour later that Sergeant Sutherland and Ross struck out for the island of Shivinish. Ross felt that the winds were not yet abating but the snowfall was definitely less dense. Navigation was hard as everywhere simply looked white, but Ross had brought an OS map along with him and was working off the headlands he saw and a general rule of heading west. Unsure of what he would find, Ross thought about how he would handle the Arnold family. How much could he tell them? Was their boy missing? If so, would they simply want to go to him, or maybe search for him? The burnt body in the morgue would be almost impossible to identify visually.

As the pair crested a small summit, Ross saw a white path down to a section of beach that connected one island to the other. But the tide had not receded that far, and he thought he might have about three to four hours at best, risk free, to make it back over. The Arnolds would no doubt know better.

Peering through the snowfall, which was being driven into his face, Ross swore he could see someone on the far side of the sands. He waved his arms above him in hope of some acknowledgement, but none was forthcoming. Maybe the person was not even looking his direction. Tom had spotted the person as well and was making even more exaggerated efforts in vain.

But seeing the other person had renewed their drive for the new island, the pair almost running down the slope, to make their way onto a short stretch of sand. At first, Ross's feet sank and he tepidly tried to find firmer sand before striding out across the freshly revealed bank. It was not lost on Ross the uniqueness of this moment. Although he had seen snow at the beach before, never had he crossed between two white lands on a pale, yellow bridge and looking both ways, he tried to drink in the moment.

On arrival at the other side, he realised the figure had moved away and he looked for a sign of habitation on this smaller island. Tracing the coastline, Ross saw a small harbour and a batch of buildings near it.

'That must be the Arnolds,' said Ross. 'We made good time. And there's his fishing boat.'

Tom Sutherland seemed calmer now he had the boat in sight. Something about the man made Ross think he was unreliable but to voice such a thing would only make matters worse. Maybe Tom was just out of his depth of experience. Ross certainly was.

The clump of houses were three barns and a house with two stories. Making straight for the front door, Ross hammered it, desperate to get inside and out of the wind. The door was opened by a woman in a large jumper and jeans. Her face was a picture and she seemed stunned for a moment.

'DC Ross and Sergeant Sutherland, ma'am. I'm guessing you're Mrs Arnold. Can we come in; it'll be easier to talk?'

Stepping back and waving them inside, the woman shouted for 'David'. Then she took the coats of the officers and ushered them inside to sit in front of stove. The heat of the room was oppressive after being out in the cold, but Ross was not complaining.

'Sorry to bother you, ma'am, but there's been a spot of bother on the main island and we need to contact the mainland, Mrs Arnold.'

'It's June, Detective; please call me June. My husband David is coming, and you can see some of the kids peering around the doors. We don't get many visitors.' A small boy ran up to June Arnold and clung to her legs. 'And this is my youngest, Jack.'

Ross went to smile at the child, but a man walked in and stood looking at the officers with a dark suspicion. 'Don't get many here. What's the trouble? You could have called ahead.'

'Sorry to bother, sir, DC Ross and Sergeant Sutherland. Unfortunately, there's been several deaths on the main island, and we need to use your vessel to call the mainland. There's a girl in a medically awkward situation and she could do with being airlifted off.'

'Well, by all means you can use the radio, but I am not taking the vessel out of the harbour in this weather. Be bloody dangerous. It's not the largest boat in the world.'

'Of course, sir. Just the radio. By the way, is the whole of your family here?'

The man shrugged his shoulders. 'Our Debbie and Alan are both eighteen-plus, so they wander where they want. I'm not sure if they made it in here before the storm. There's another smaller abode on the other side of the island and sometimes they might go there to get their own space. But Jack's here.' The man looked at his wife who shrugged her shoulders too. Then he shouted for his children. 'Debbie! Alan! Kylie!'

A young woman swung around the door. She had a heavily made-up face and was wearing leggings with a t-shirt. The

143

woman stared up and down at Ross before giving the same treatment to Sutherland.

'Don't mind Debbie, Constable, she's like that with everyone. A recluse. Have you seen Alan or Kylie, Debs?'

'Kylie's upstairs. Alan hasn't been in since yesterday.'

'I did see someone when I crossed the beach,' offered Ross.

'Probably him then,' said June, 'likes his own company. Do you want something, Constable, or do you want to get straight to the boat? You've got about three hours before you need to cross back or you'll be staying the night.'

'Let's get to the boat in case there's any involved messages or they need me to wait on a call back. If you'll accompany me, Mr Arnold.'

'Of course, Detective, I'll just get my coat.' The man returned in a large fluorescent jacket complete with a balaclava on his head. As a fisherman, Ross reckoned the man would be prepared for the worst of weather and so it seemed. Looking down at the man's boots, Ross felt jealous and dreamed of placing his bare feet in a hot bath when all of this was over. But for now, he braced himself for another trip out into the cold.

The harbour was small but well-built and Ross saw that the fishing vessel was barely moving despite the crash of the waves from beyond the artificial structure. Mr Arnold led the way and seemed to simply hop along the harbour wall before letting himself down onto his boat. Ross was much more careful as he descended a ladder before racing into the wheelhouse clear of the storm.

'Just the one set, although I do have a handheld as well, but you'll be lucky to get anyone on it. Do you want to do the call or should I?' asked David Arnold.

'Maybe best if you call it, sir, and then I can speak to them once the communications are made.'

'As you wish, Detective. Is this a distress situation or merely some trouble? It's just you haven't said yet.'

'It's urgent and you need to get through, Mr Arnold. Just make sure you get through to them.'

Ross watched the man chew over what had been said and then fire up his radio. The call went out to the Stornoway Coastguard and Ross heard the man explain he had a police officer wishing to contact the authorities. There was some debate about whether or not a mobile could be used and then Ross watched the man change a dial and speak to someone different.

'That's them ready for you, Detective. All you need to do is press the button when you talk. Leave it off when you want to hear. It's that simple.' Ross had used a radio before but he did not take offence.

'Hello, Coastguard, this is Constable Ross, over.'

'This is Stornoway Coastguard; how can we be of assistance?'

Ross wondered how much he should put out over the airwaves, but maybe the best thing was to stress the urgency and medical help needed for Kiera Harris. After detailing her injuries and her current status, he was put into a call with a medical doctor. There seemed to be question after question and Ross really had no idea what Lucy had done to help Kiera. Had she given medication? He doubted it but maybe she had basic medical supplies, paracetamol, and the like.

In the end, the call took over twenty minutes and he was advised that a helicopter would be on its way. Ross was able to give a grid reference for the casualty's position and he was told to expect the helicopter in about an hour or so. Maybe a touch longer given the current weather.

After the call was complete, Ross joined Mr Arnold back in his house and accepted a quick cup of tea. The sweet liquid could be felt descending his cold throat and he took the opportunity to ask the man about how he came to the island.

'It's just a good gig, Detective, especially as far as fishing's concerned. The boy and I go out every once in a while, and we get paid whatever we bring in. It's the same rate whatever we land. They say that it goes to that Viscount's restaurants and that. Best of fish he claims, but there's nothing special about what we're landing. It's good fish but like anywhere else.'

'And do you land it on the islands across from here? I mean the Western Isles.'

'No, not many places there to land them on the Uists but even if I wanted to, the Viscount likes me to drop them off on Ceann Iar, to Celeste and Hamish. They do a boat run every so often and drop the fish on the mainland. It's a fair old trip as they have to round Barra and then take them into Oban. All-day trip there and an all-day back really.'

'Do you see them often, Celeste and Hamish?'

'Usually only when I drop the fish off, or you see Hamish going up to the main community every once in a while. Goes well prepared, mind, has a rucksack on his back, maybe his lunch inside. Comes back with it still fully loaded. Probably supplies for the main island.'

'Is that what you do as well, travel over for your supplies?' asked Ross, warming himself by the stove.

'No, we're very self-sufficient. When Hamish comes back from the mainland, he brings us whatever we need, and we simply keep ourselves to ourselves. It's good money but the family are bored. Especially when the Wi-Fi goes and that, the older kids especially just get fed up.'

'Modern times, I guess. We didn't have internet growing up. Made your own fun.' Ross downed his tea. 'Thank you, Mr Arnold, and before we leave, we will let you know exactly what has happened, but I would recommend your family stay on this island.'

'That's very cryptic and a bit worrying.'

'Yes sir, it is, but I make no apology.'

With that Ross departed with Tom Sutherland to make their journey back to the community hall on the other island. As they left the Arnold's they saw a figure ahead in the snow. It disappeared after they crested a hill and Ross put it down to the Arnold's son, Alan. One thing that bothered Ross was that he had no definite proof of where the man was, but his parents had been pretty confident that he was on their island, stashed away in the second abode. Well, there was too much going on to worry about that now. Crossing the sands again, Ross felt his steps becoming lighter now that he knew help was on the way.

The trip seemed shorter too and Tom Sutherland bright despite the cold. The snow had now stopped but they still had to fight through the thick layer that lay on the ground. As they approached the hall from the west, Ross got a sudden sinking feeling in his gut as he saw the main door was lying open.

'Tom, look! The door's open. Allen's not daft enough to have opened it to anyone, is he?'

'No,' replied the man and the Sergeant seemed to begin to stamp his feet. 'He can't have.' Tom began to run but Ross caught hold of his arm.

'Wait! We have no idea what's going on there. You could walk right into something. We need to approach quietly and check everything.' The Sergeant nodded but drew his nightstick. Ross felt somewhat more exposed not having a weapon but still found himself taking the lead as they approached the door.

Ross crept forward slowly, glancing inside through the glass panes. He saw someone at a chair by the small kitchen area. The panelling that had separated the temporary morgue from the rest of the hall was knocked over and Ross struggled to see a body on the table. Slowly he made his way through the door and keep low as he came through the hall. The mattress where Kiera had been lying was just out of view and Ross stopped himself from rushing forward to discover if the woman was all right.

'Can you see anything?' The stage whisper from Tom was not helpful and Ross braced himself for an attack from the edges of the room. But no one came and Ross got closer to the figure in the chair. It was Allen and he was bent over, doubled in what must have been an incredibly uncomfortable position. And that meant, he was probably dead. The blood dripping from the man's neck indicated as much.

Ross could now hear the Sergeant approaching behind him and as he turned around, Ross saw the man move out of a low crouch and walk briskly toward the chair containing Constable Allen. As if Ross was not there, the man walked clean past and then placed a hand on Allen's shoulder. Ross saw the head swing to one side and realised the neck had been badly severed, to the point that the head was struggling to stay attached.

Now that Sutherland had blown their stealthy approach, Ross raced around the building and checked for any intruders, but the building was silent and devoid of movement. Only then did he check where Kiera Harris had been sleeping. The blankets covering the woman were in a mess and covered in blood. Pulling them back, Ross saw a body that could not maintain life such were the injuries. Kiera Harris was definitely deceased and her death must have been brutal.

His heart raced as he span around searching the room for one more body but he found none. He slowly checked every corner again and then returned to the toilet where he saw that the high window was open. Lucy was young and agile. She just might have gone that way. Ross prayed she had. Just maybe, she might have escaped.

Chapter 17

Macleod hung up the call on his mobile and smiled. His team were getting somewhere but he was just not sure where. Without any call from Ross, he was still in the dark about what was happening on the island. But Kirsten seemed to have come up trumps with the mainland side of things. Amanda Novak had been a partner to Bonnar, a fancy woman or kept pet, something of that ilk and now she had been taken away or left him for someone else. And she had gotten involved with drugs. But how had that taken her to the island. As a drug tester, a live specimen to play on? Did Bonnar know, or was he just hacked off at having his girl taken from him.

And then there was Mary Flaherty. Was it too much of a jump to suspect she might be Kiera Harris? She had gotten heavily involved with drugs and then ended up going with a posher girl, one not from the drug dens. Was she taken to the island? A sea of thoughts and connotations flowed around Macleod's head and he knew he needed to see the lie of the land before he could get a real grip on what was happening.

The other interesting aspect was that Donoghue had gone to ground or at least was not where his diary said he should be. Macleod had thought about involving himself in bringing

Donoghue to the light and then interviewing him, but his gut kept saying he had to get to the Monach Islands.

As he strolled from the airport for the third time that day, he saw a number he did not recognise. 'Macleod.'

'Detective Inspector, this is the Aeronautical Rescue Co-ordination Centre.'

'The people who send the helicopters?'

'That's us, sir. You were previously asking about the Monach Islands and getting to there with one of our helos. Well, we, that is the coastguard, have just received an urgency message regarding a casualty on the Monach Islands. It was called in by a DC Ross. I thought you had best be informed. He also has stated that he now had two deceased persons and one requiring medical attention. We are sending a rescue helicopter out of Prestwick.'

'You need to get me on that helicopter. When's it departing?'

The next five minutes were a negotiation between Macleod and the senior officer at the co-ordination centre where Macleod laid out his belief that his officer was in immediate need of support due to the dangerous circumstances. After giving assurances that the crew would not be in danger and assuring that two officers would also accompany him, Macleod was asked to get to Prestwick as soon as possible.

In the taxi, he arranged for two officers to be available at the helicopter to accompany him. As the taxi raced on, Macleod rang Hope to advise her of the situation.

'I'll head there directly,' she advised.

'No! You stay and catch up with Kirsten. There are two places where things might happen, the islands and the mainland. Clearly there's something between Bonnar and Donoghue so I need you here to get on top of that. Check in with Jona when she gets the fish, she might have some line of attack for you to follow.'

'The fish, sir?'

'Got to go, Hope. Ask Kirsten about her fish.'

It was only as the taxi pulled into Prestwick airport that Macleod realised he had left his wellington boots in the car that Hope was driving. His feet were about to get cold.

* * *

Ross wondered what he should do. Lucy was out there somewhere. But the land was fairly flat and she should be visible, especially now that the snow was dissipating. But then again, if she had escaped, she could be in hiding. And if she had not, then she could be held out of sight. Or worse.

He thought about a discussion with Tom Sutherland, but the man was having a breakdown. Kneeling down before his half-decapitated partner, he was weeping like a baby and muttering about things he had said to the younger man. If Ross were to leave the community hall then he wanted to be sure he could move about quietly.

But maybe staying put was the realistic option. Maybe to wait for the helo would be the sensible option. Lock the door. But had the door not been locked before. So, someone had a key. Or Allen had let someone he thought no threat in.

If the helo arrived, then there was no body to take away. But it could search the island surely. Didn't they have cameras? Maybe he could signal his troubles before they got close and warn them. But who was he warning them about? Who had done this? And why?

Ross felt vulnerable right where he was and decided he needed to be outside the building somewhere he could see anyone come and go. Whether Tom would come was another issue. Grabbing the man's arm, Ross urged the Sergeant to follow him, but the man kept crying and pushed Ross away. There was nothing for it. Ross could best protect the man by watching over him from outside. But he would lock the door for what it was worth.

Before he left, Ross explained what he was going to do but Tom Sutherland would not listen and kept staring at the body of PC Allen. A breakdown had been on the cards even before this horror and now Tom was in one up to his neck. It was a painful decision, but Ross had to do what it took to stay alive and to hopefully find Lucy.

Grabbing a blanket, Ross stepped outside looking this way and that before locking the door behind him and running across the field to the nearest slope he could find and then burying himself in the snow. He used the blanket as a barrier between the snow and himself, but it was proving to be a mistake as it got wet extremely quickly.

As he settled down to watch the community hall from a short distance away, Ross was also able to look across at the small settlement and the square where it all started. There was the still smouldering wreck of Amanda Novak's house but there was no Paul Kemp outside. Settling back down and quietly watching the community hall, Ross noted a line of broken snow and what looked like possible footprints coming away from the rear of the hall. They would be close to the toilet and the open window he had found.

Something inside him said, *Wait, there's a helicopter on its way and you can then look safely from above.* But the police officer

153

in him determined that if Lucy were alive she would need his help and that could not wait whatever the danger. He laid his blanket out flat as a target for the helicopter and then ran across to the footprints he had seen.

Sure enough, they were daintier feet than his and he reckoned they must belong to Lucy. They led across the island and ran right to its middle where they seemed to stop. At least he could see them disappear into the distance. As he got closer, he saw a metal grid on the ground. It was a sewage drain or some sort of collection unit for waste perhaps. Ross realised he did not really know but rather than berate his lack of knowledge, Ross decided to try the grid. It opened easily and he looked inside.

He recoiled, recognising the smell of rotten fish. But why was there rotting fish down here anyway. Replacing the grid again, Ross wondered what Lucy did once she reached here. Had she tried to hide in the apparent sewer? Maybe she had fallen in. Had she been unlucky? Maybe someone threw her in? He had no way of knowing and the lack of sleep was not making his brain sharp today.

Ross went back to his blanket and lay down on it in the snow. He lifted his head occasionally to try and hear but above the noise of the wind he heard nothing. But then he felt a vibration and heard a sound that brought a joy to his heart. He scanned the horizon but struggled to locate what was making such a din. Then it reared up from the sea, lifting up and over the rocks by the eastern cliffs. The red and white machine dominated the scene and Ross jumped up and waved his hands like crazy. At last, he had someone to help, someone to approach for assistance. The helicopter came close to the ground blowing up a snowstorm and Ross saw a figure jump out with a large, black helmet. And then another figure joined it. There was a long overcoat and then a gait that spoke of his inspector.

* * *

'Over there, that's Ross. He's the one who contacted us,' shouted Macleod over the noise of the aircraft.

Together they rushed over to his officer who was staggering towards them. Macleod read a face that showed relief but also a degree of hesitation in what was about to come. 'Ross, are you all right? Alan?'

'Sir, Lucy is missing, my forensic lead. I had to get the message out to you and while I was away, someone killed Allen, the island constable, and Lucy's gone. They also killed Kiera Harris.'

'Where are the bodies?' asked the paramedic quickly. He knew it was a protocol, the paramedic would not see them as deceased until he had verified it. Ross pointed to a hall and Macleod placed an arm around his officer, telling the paramedic to wait.

'Dave, I've got murdered people in there. I know you want to get to them in case they are still alive, but I can't say it's safe. Let me go in first. You stay behind me with Ross. If anything happens, go straight back into the helicopter and get out of here. Understand, you don't wait for me.' Macleod saw the man's face go pale, but he seemed resolute enough.

Transferring Ross to the paramedic, Macleod walked slowly towards the community hall looking around. The white snow set the building up on a perfect pedestal and the backdrop of the sea in the distance would have made this a terrific tourist advert. But Macleod could see the chaos inside. He turned and waved for the two accompanying policemen to come out. The officers ran over to Macleod and he briefed them on the situation.

'I want you to accompany me, Hughes. Finlay, get back in the helicopter and protect the crew. You have my permission to depart if things go wrong but I want you to try and get this paramedic out at worst. I'm not sure what we've walked into here but be prepared for weapons.'

Hughes was a strapping constable, sporting a thick Glasgow accent and a mop of blonde hair. But his face was focused and grim as he reached the door of the hall with Macleod. Trying it, he turned to the Inspector indicating it was locked.

'I have a key,' said Ross, offering it to Macleod. 'Sergeant Sutherland's inside, sir. And it's not a good sight. He's broken down. Last I saw of him he was kneeling before his colleague who's almost decapitated. Sorry, sir, it's a mess.'

Macleod wanted to take Ross to one side and explain it was not his fault, that he had done well given the circumstances. The man needed bolstering. Although Macleod was sure Ross was glad to see him, Macleod was his senior and Ross would expect to have to explain the situation. Given the current state of affairs, that would never be easy, and Ross would question everything he had done in the days ahead. It was par for the course when lives were lost.

Macleod opened the door and Hughes stepped cautiously inside. Macleod then flanked the man and together they began to search the building. On the floor, still crying was a well-built policeman, presumably Sergeant Sutherland, and in front of him was a body that had slumped forward in a chair, its head slightly cocked to one side revealing a gap where the neck should have seamlessly joined.

Stepping past the scene, Macleod and Hughes swept the rest of the building. 'No one. Dave, do what you need to do. Hughes, lock that front door and stand guard. You see anyone but the helo crew or your colleague, I want you to holler.'

Hughes made for the door, but Macleod saw the man's face and it was becoming more like the snow. Sometimes Macleod forgot he was *used* to these types of scenes. The paramedic was also well versed as he had no hesitation in checking out the unfortunate constable and then the other bodies before quickly moving back to Sergeant Sutherland as the only living person requiring treatment. Macleod walked around the scene with Ross.

'This is the temporary morgue Lucy set up,' said Ross, shaking, and probably not from the cold. 'The first body is Amanda Novak, and she was killed with a long thin weapon, but it was made to look like a suicide. The Sergeant got suspicious with the lack of blood from her cut wrists, that's why we're here.'

Macleod knew this but he thought it best to let Ross talk, let a degree of normality resume, reporting to his senior as he did every day. But the Inspector was under no illusions. This was not a simple crime scene. The brutality of the killing of the constable and the distance they were from help was giving him serious cause for concern.

'The charred body came from a fire that was started last night in Amanda Novak's house. It's been burnt to a crisp, sir. I pulled Kiera Harris from that fire, too. She was alive but not in a good way. After the fire, I decided to pull the team into here and lock us down. But we needed to get away and Kiera Harris needed assistance. So, I went with the mayor and the Sergeant to the communications hut on the other end of this island. The place was damaged beyond our repair. When I came back, I then made for Shivinish, the middle island, to speak to the Arnolds and use their boat to contact the coastguard. When I got back, Allen was dead and so was Kiera Harris. Lucy was missing and I think she made a run for it from the footprints I found leaving from underneath the toilet window.'

'Okay, Ross, you did good. Take photographs, fast. I'm clearing out of here very soon; I don't think we are safe here.'

'But you can't leave Lucy behind, Seoras. She's out there alone.'

Macleod felt his arm being grabbed and saw the terror in Ross's eyes. The man had done well to hold it together so far, but the stress and the lack of sleep were telling. He needed to put his head down for a few hours, at the very least.

'Easy, Ross. We'll get her but we need to secure the safety of everyone. Take the photos and then we'll get the deceased off to the helicopter. I need to talk to Dave about the Sergeant and then I'll give you a hand. Remember the helicopter came out to rush someone to hospital. Unfortunately, Kiera won't be needing that so I think these guys can do what they are trained for and look for Lucy.'

Ross went quiet but his arm still gripped Macleod. Gently he pushed his junior officer into a chair and told him to simply sit there. Tapping Dave on the shoulder, he asked the paramedic to take a look at Ross when he could.

There was a reason Macleod always asked someone else to take photos of crime scenes if forensics were not there and that was due to his ineptness with a camera. But he knew what he wanted in the photographs so he did not bother Hughes on the door. Once Dave had examined both officers, he advised

Macleod that they should be removed from the scene and taken somewhere to be looked after. Neither was in any serious danger, just shocked.

'Good, Dave, thank you. We have a missing colleague out there and I'm going to need your crew's assistance. But we need to get everyone somewhere safe. I also have a duty to try and protect the people on this island and get an investigation going.' Macleod turned to Ross. 'Where's safe, Ross? Where can we set up a better base?' Ross hung his head despondently. 'Constable, get your head up. It might look bleak but right now I need you firing on all cylinders. You've been here. Is the other island an option?'

'The Arnolds might be good. I don't think they are involved. They did let us get a signal out.'

'Excellent. Dave, radio your crew. We're going to put all the victims in body bags and load them onto the helo. From there we will move to the Arnold's house on Shivinish. After I establish a base, we're going to go looking for our missing colleague. I reckon you could cover these islands in no time.'

The paramedic put the plan in to action and ten minutes later, the helicopter was fully loaded, the bodies of the victims safely stowed, and the rest of the remaining team now strapped in their seats. The helicopter was not far from full capacity as it lifted into the rapidly clearing air. As it rose above the islands, Macleod saw the black mark of the burnt down house among the main settlement on the island. But there was no one about. Maybe they were hiding, in fear for their lives. Or maybe they were in on it.

Chapter 18

Kirsten Stewart strode into the Inverness station and made her way directly to the forensic department. After giving a brief knock on the door, she ignored the stares of those working in the lab and went straight for Jona Nakamura's office. Another quick knock on the door was followed by a polite 'Come in' and Stewart gave a broad smile to the Asian officer behind her desk.

'Hi. I thought you guys were off to the Monach Islands. I haven't heard back from Lucy—'

'Regarding that,' interrupted Stewart and slapping a fish in a bag onto Jona's desk, 'I need to know the difference between this fish, and this one.' Stewart plonked the second fish in the evidence bag beside the first one.

'Well, they are the same species and roughly the same size. There's not a lot I can tell without taking them out and doing a proper examination. There are a few other things on the go at the moment. Can you give me a day or so?'

'If you can, Jona, can you do it now? I've a feeling it's going to come up with something big.'

'How so?' asked the Japanese woman taking the bags in two hands and nodding to indicate that Stewart should get the door.

'One fish comes courtesy of the Viscount Donoghue estate for my lunch, and the other comes from a crate of fish he decided not to give me. I want to know what's so special about that fish. They are all coming back from a small fishing operation on the Monach Islands, but my guide was keen to get me a special fish to take away. I'm guessing that one will turn out to be great when fried but nothing else. The other . . .'

'Well, let's find out,' said Jona and walked into the lab and called her team over. Stewart took the chance to step away from the impromptu meeting. Jona ran her team and was the boss to the forensic division. Maybe Macleod or McGrath might join the discussion uninvited, but Stewart always left Jona to her own team.

A few minutes later, Jona came back to Stewart and asked for an hour. Recognising the poorly disguised request for Stewart to get out and let the team get on with it, Kirsten made her way to the canteen, famished as she was after her drive. As she sat enjoying some lasagne, a call came on her mobile.

'Kirsten, it's Hope. Where are you?'

'Back at the station. What do you need?'

'Nothing, I'm on my way up and was just looking to touch base. The boss has gone over to the island so we should hopefully get an update on what he's doing shortly. Until then, you and I have the job of understanding who took Kiera Harris to the island. Although we might get that answer from Kiera if they can get her to a hospital in time. She was in a bad way after a fire.'

'Any word of Ross?' The worry in Stewart's voice was evident.

'He's okay last I heard but had his hands full. The boss still thinks there's something occurring on the island to have caused the death of Amanda Novak and now this. But he's only got his gut instinct, no proof.'

'Well, I think I might have something on that. I've been to the Donoghue estate and I've seen the warehouse they use for the island. There's a lot of impressive machinery and parts there in crates. They also bring fish back for the island and I have two being cut up by Jona as we speak. I'm awaiting her results.'

'Good, I'll be with you in an hour and we can make our next steps. Hopefully, we'll have heard from the boss and make a sensible line of attack. In the meantime, see if you can get into any accounts for that island and the items that have been purchased. See if any stand out as unusual for an eco-island, or a place of peace and quiet.'

'Yes, boss.' The call closed and Kirsten looked at the half-eaten lasagne before her. There was salad with it and a few chips, and her stomach was growling for it. Picking the plate up, she made her way back the office. There was no way she was going to work on an empty stomach.

* * *

There was a flurry of snow as the helo landed a short distance to the west of the Arnold's house. Macleod could see a man running from the building, wrapped up in a fisherman's coat and trousers. He seemed to be in utter wonder at the mechanical beast and Macleod was keen to greet the man, but the inspector sat in his seat until the rear crew gave him the

162

okay to exit the helicopter.

Ross jumped out ahead of the Inspector and shook hands with David Arnold and introduced him to Macleod. As the rotors wound down, Mr Arnold suggested they enter the house. Macleod turned to the helicopter crew and asked that one of the pilots stay on board, ready to start the helicopter if necessary. Constable Finlay was also tasked to remain as protection while Hughes assisted Sergeant Sutherland to the house. As the small party entered, they were greeted by June Arnold and two of her children.

'This is Debbie and Kylie, Inspector. Jack's my wee one and he's playing upstairs. I don't suppose you've seen Alan. I suspect he's in the small building on the other side of our island. Sometimes he hides out there.'

'I'm sorry,' said Macleod shaking the woman's hand, 'but I haven't. I intend to search these islands from the helicopter so I will look for your son. May we use your kitchen table. There's a lot to discuss and we need to get back in the air before the light starts to go.'

Within five minutes, the table hosted a small conference of Macleod, Ross, Sutherland and Hughes from the police, the captain of the helicopter, Diggs, Dave, his winchman and paramedic and Dave and June Arnold. Clutching a hot cup of tea, Macleod looked at the assembly and began.

'This is quite unprecedented but I'm highly unsure just who is involved on Ceann Ear in the events that have happened. Because of this, we treat everyone from there as potentially hostile. Given that someone has killed four people so far, we need to be careful. Therefore, I'm confining your crew to the helo once we are airborne, Captain Diggs. You don't stop the rotors running for anything, even if we land. What's the best way for us to search from the air, Captain?'

'We can conduct a search from the air using the cameras and our FLIR cameras. In the snow we should get good images, but they will only tell you so much. You may need to get out and investigate. There's also a fuel issue. We weren't planning for a search so can maybe look for an hour, maybe a bit longer depending on how we search, and then we need to go to Benbecula to refuel. I'm happy to do that and return but you need to be aware. If you are on the main island during that time, we can't come get you.'

'Then I'd suggest we don't stay on that island without any reinforcements,' said Macleod. 'I suggest that Sergeant Sutherland remains here and rests up. Hughes can stay here as protection for the house and as a contact point. Do we have any radios in the house?'

'Not in the house, Inspector, but I do have a handheld in the boat. That should be picked up by the helicopter,' suggested David Arnold, and Captain Diggs agreed.

'I also suggest we keep our victims on the helicopter until we are able to bring them to suitable facilities. Ross, if you're up to it, you will join me on the helo. That way there'll be three of us to protect the helo and occupants. When we have to get off the aircraft, you and I will do the searching and Finlay will stay on board. If we have need of a paramedic and it's safe, Dave can join us.

'Mrs Arnold, my apologies for imposing on you but does that sound okay to you? Sergeant Sutherland could do with a couch and a few blankets.'

'Of course, Inspector. I shall get organised.' As the woman left the room, Mr Arnold coughed abruptly before turning to Macleod.

164

'I think I should join you in the helo. It is my son you are looking for.'

Macleod held up his hands in an apologetic fashion. 'I'm sorry, sir, it's too risky. I won't have you out of the helo with me due to the danger involved. And as to staying on the helo, that's a bad idea to my mind as well but it is the captain's call.'

Captain Diggs stood up and also looked apologetic. 'I know it's your boy but, sir, you will be in the way. Let us do our jobs. Please.'

David Arnold looked far from happy, but he did not push the issue much to Macleod's delight. There was enough happening without involving civilians. Macleod drained his tea and started to chivvy everyone to their task. The light was beginning to fade and Macleod stepped out into a chilling wind, yet the sky was almost clear. There would be a frost tonight but not a snowfall. And if Lucy were outside in it, the poor girl would struggle to survive.

The helicopter lifted in a blur of snow and Macleod tried to relax in his seat while Captain Digg's crew went to work. From his seat Macleod could see one of the crew looking at several screens and then zooming in and out with cameras. They passed over the houses of the main settlement and Macleod could see heat signatures in the houses.

'Is there any way to count those people in the houses? I mean can you recognise a person in that mesh of colour?' Macleod was talking on the internal communications and pointing at the screen which showed yellow, blues and reds in a blend. The hotspots showed the houses, even Macleod could spot that, but he could not pick out the detail of any persons.

'I can give it a go,' said the camera operator and Macleod saw he was joined by Dave the paramedic as they looked for patterns in the colours.

'I believe the house below us has one person in it,' said the cameraman.

'That's Orla and Kiera's house. There would be only one person,' replied Ross to Macleod's look.

'And this house has two.'

'That's the mayor,' announced Ross. 'Just his daughter Autumn and him.'

'No one in that one.'

'That should be Paul and Daniella. Where the hell are they?' asked Ross.

'And the last one has three in it,' finished the cameraman.

'Three? That's the oldies,' said Ross. 'Alfie and Edna Collins. He was rather abrupt too. What's he doing with someone else in there?'

'It's worth a shot. Captain, can we land near the settlement and we'll go take a call at the Collins. Keep the rotors running and I'll keep Constable Finlay at the door of the helo for protection.'

Macleod found his stomach churning as he waited for the helicopter to land. It was an enormous beast and sent the snow into a flurry. Once the aircraft had touched down, the sliding door was opened, and he accompanied Ross to the house of Alfie and Edna Collins.

There were lights on inside and Ross first checked the large window of the living room before coming back to Macleod. 'They're watching television. It's like nothing's happened or is happening. I don't understand.'

'Well, we'll find out why they're so chilled out.' Macleod rapped the door loudly. There was no movement in the hallway and Macleod rapped it again. Again no one came. So

Macleod strode to the window and thumped it so hard, Ross reckoned he could have easily smashed the window. 'Open up, Mr Collins, or I'll kick the door down. You might be in danger!'

Macleod could see Alfie Collins rising somewhat nonchalantly and then make for the hallway. The light came on and Macleod was standing on the small step when Mr Collins opened the door.

'Detective Inspector Macleod, sir. Who is in your house?'

'Who the blazes are you? And are you back?' asked the man looking with disdain at Ross.

'Sir, who is in your house?' thundered Macleod. When the man did not answer, he brushed past him and began to tear through to the kitchen. 'Ross, check upstairs.' Macleod heard Alfie Collins following him, the man chuntering away about civil rights. 'Your life may be in danger, Mr Collins. I am bound to take this action in my role as a police officer.'

Opening the kitchen door, Macleod fumbled for a light switch. As it came on, he swore somebody raced out of the back door. 'Ross, he's outside.' Running out of the back door, Macleod was caught in the stomach by a punch and doubled over immediately. A second blow caught him on the back. But then there was nothing as his attacker fled. It was the sound of Ross careering though the kitchen that must have done it. By the time Macleod looked up, he could not see anyone.

'Are you okay, sir?'

'Yes, Ross,' replied Macleod taking in deep breaths of air. 'Just a bit of a rough punch but I'm okay. But he got away. If we get back to the helo we might just be able to see him in the open.' Leaving Alfie Collins where he was standing and complaining quite heavily, the pair raced back to the helo. A quick word to the cameraman meant they were airborne two minutes later. Macleod scanned the cameras from his seat but saw nothing.

'Is anyone seeing anything?' asked Macleod.

'Negative,' said the cameraman.

'And, Inspector, we have an issue. I need to go and get fuel in five minutes. What do you want to do?'

Before he could answer, Dave the paramedic interrupted. 'Look at that. That piece of ground should be dark. There's something warm under there.'

Macleod looked at the screen and saw the large rectangle that was showing up red. It was not the hottest signature, but they seemed to find it strange.

'The normal camera's not showing anything there,' said Dave's colleague in the rear of the aircraft.

'Are you investigating it, Inspector,' asked Captain Diggs, 'because I need to go?'

Macleod thought about this. If he didn't investigate it could be maybe two hours before they get back here. Lucy could still be out there and maybe this was a shelter for her. But it was a risk with a murderer running around.

'She could be out there, sir,' said Ross.

'Indeed, she could. Are you happy to go?' Ross nodded. 'Finlay, you happy to stay with us?' The man nodded. 'Right then, grab a torch and whatever else we need. Captain, drop us at your earliest convenience. And by the way, do you have a handheld radio?'

A minute later, Macleod was standing in deep snow, looking at the departing helicopter. The lights of the settlement were nearby but they did little to light up the darkness that stretched before Macleod. The captain had said he should walk about one hundred metres from where they had dropped them to find the unusual heat signature. Switching on his torch, Macleod strode off in the correct direction, determined to find something before freezing out here.

His back-up plan, if he found nothing, was to head back to the Collins's for shelter until the helo came back. He could certainly overpower Collins if he were the murderer but having seen the man, he wondered if Collins really had the strength.

As Macleod approached the area, he swept his torch beam back and forward, trying to find something in the now-dark vista. But there was nothing. He walked to and fro, stamping as if he should be able to find something.

'Nothing Ross, absolutely nothing. So where did our runner go to? They couldn't just vanish into mid-air. Anyway, we can't stay here too long, or we'll freeze. Let's go. Macleod turned round and began to walk to the settlement when he heard Constable Finlay cry out as he fell.

'Are you okay, Finlay?'

'Yes, Inspector, I think I am. But my foot caught something.'

Macleod shined a light on where Finlay had fallen, seeing hastily thrown snow and an attempt to cover up something underneath. Kicking the snow aside, Macleod found a small domed entrance and a wheeled handle to open it, somewhat like the top of a submarine. Grabbing the wheel enthusiastically, Macleod turned it as fast as he could. He heard a release of pressure and then threw open the curved lid.

A pungent stench hit his nostrils and he struggled not to rear away from it. But instead, he carefully shone his light inside. In the depths he could see a brown liquid and a ladder disappearing down the wall and then into the sludge at the bottom of the drop.

'It's an effluent site. I guess,' said Ross.

'Maybe,' said Macleod, 'but it's also somewhere warm for anyone who needs shelter. Think about it, Ross. Who's going to come looking for you in the rubbish, especially stinking like this?'

'Shall I go down first?'

'No, I'll do it Ross. But keep your eyes peeled. We could be walking right into where the killer wants us. Macleod took a last breath of the fresh air beyond the opening and then began to step down the ladder. He held his breath, and then took in lungfuls via his mouth when necessary. Descending, he reached a small platform and looked around him. Where was his killer? Where was Lucy?

From the corner of his eye, Macleod saw that the wall was not quite perfect but had a line running down it. Walking over, Macleod gently pushed the wall where the seam occurred. It swung open and he heard gunfire as the wall behind him exploded in a pile of dust.

Chapter 19

Macleod threw himself to one side of the platform as he saw an arm emerge through the door. The sound of the gunfire had nearly deafened him, and he struggled to maintain his balance as a woman burst through. She was dressed in a green jumper with jeans and had tied-back curly brown hair, but it was the eyes that made Macleod realise he was as good as dead. There was that hunger for death in them that he had seen in many killers, especially at the point of kill. And she was too far away from him to even try and reach her with a kick.

A shadow fell across him having tumbled from above. The woman clattered to the floor with Ross on top of her and Macleod saw someone emerging from the door. Without waiting to see who it was, Macleod charged with his shoulder down and caught a man in the stomach. Together they sprawled backwards through the door and Macleod tried to right himself from the floor. But his foe held him, and Macleod felt himself being turned over.

Macleod was not the strongest of officers and he wished he had Stewart or McGrath with him. Ross, whilst younger, always seemed to be someone who avoided the fight and managed to turn situations around without violence. But now, the pair of them were in a fight for their lives. As Macleod was turned over, he knew his side of the fight was not going well. He caught a glimpse of a young man's face as his opponent raised himself up and looked to bring his fists down onto Macleod's face. The Inspector tried to raise his hands in defence, but they were trapped by the man's legs and the dark-haired individual gave a wicked grin as he prepared to pummel Macleod.

Someone grabbed the man from behind and he saw an arm snake around the man's neck, choking him. With a heave, the man was pulled backwards off Macleod, but he was struggling like crazy. And then whoever was doing the pulling seemed to fall over as the grappling pair went back out through the door. Regaining his feet, Macleod saw Finlay on the floor with the male attacker and Ross struggling with the female assailant, their hands fighting for a gun. It was in the woman's grasp, but Ross was holding her wrist upright, meaning the gun was pointing to the ceiling.

'Aidez-moi!' shouted the woman with the gun and Macleod saw her partner turn and punch Finlay hard to the face, causing him to tumble down. The man then grabbed Ross and Macleod saw his Constable's hand slip from the woman's wrist and she was able to stand as Ross was engulfed by the man.

As the woman stood, she screamed at the man in French, so quickly that Macleod who had an extremely basic knowledge of the language, struggled to understand the words. But her actions were obvious as she waved an arm urging her partner to move out of the way. There was no time to think and Macleod raced forward and threw himself at the woman hitting her just under the ribs and causing her gun arm to fly upwards. A shot rang around the chamber again as Macleod fell back off the woman.

The railing of the platform was shaking as the woman was pressed against it by Macleod's attack and he saw her fight for her balance. The sectional metal pole of the railing fell away and Macleod saw the woman start to windmill her arms in an effort to stay upright. But she tumbled backwards, dropping into the dark below.

Her partner cried out after her and kicked Macleod in the ribs for his troubles before the man was hit by someone in the back. This caused him to sprawl forward and desperately grab the railing either side of where a gap had been created. But he did not stay there long as Ross delivered a kick to the man's back causing him to fall forward. There was a splash as he landed in whatever was causing the stench in the chamber.

'Paul, have you got the gun?'

The voice came from through the door Macleod had pushed open only a few moments ago but it was distant. *There must be some depth to the structure beyond, as the helicopter had indicated,* thought Macleod. There was three of them and who knew how many beyond the door. And those beyond had a firearm. There was no decision. He had stumbled upon whatever secret they hid on this island but for now the safety of his officers was paramount.

'Ross, get Finlay to his feet. We're getting out, now!'

Macleod stepped forward and closed the door to the platform, trying to add a blockage between themselves and the oncoming armed foes. Finlay was being encouraged up the short ladder to the surface and when Macleod turned, he saw Ross taking the first rungs as well. Looking around for a weapon, Macleod saw none and decided to simply get up the ladder as quick as he could behind Ross. He would be exposed if they came through the door. But if they were armed his chances were slim anyway.

His heart thundered as he climbed the ladder. Footsteps rang in his ears, coming ever closer. As he broke the surface and then threw himself forward onto the snow, a shot rang out behind him. Macleod scrambled to his feet and saw Ross grabbing the lid of the entrance and throwing it shut. Without waiting, Macleod grabbed Finlay by the arm and began to run.

But where to go, Seoras? Think man, think. If we stay out in the wilds there's little cover. And who can we trust if we go to a home. The Arnold's home was a good place, but it might put them in danger. And could they even get there? If Ross crossed earlier that day, then had twelve hours or thereabouts passed since then? Macleod was not sure. *Maybe best we take a route to an empty house and barricade ourselves. Then we could get a message on the handheld to the Arnolds or to the helicopter. This needs reinforcements now.*

Macleod dragged Finlay through the snow, the man still groggy from a hard punch. There was blood running from the man's chin and he seemed to be somewhat distant. But he was running. At least the man was running.

Ross came up alongside Macleod and took over Finlay's arm. 'Where do we go, sir? Where?'

'One of the empty houses and barricade us in. We can use the radio from there and try and get the Arnolds. Come on, Ross, they'll not be far behind us. If we can hide before they see us, it'll be for the better.'

The night air was cold and their breath formed before them as they ran. A bright moon allowed them to see their path easily and the lights of the settlement came into view quickly.

Ross steered the party around the rear of the houses before trying a rear door, finding it open.

'This is the house of Orla and Kiera, sir. To get to the empty one means we'll have to go across the square. This is probably our safest place. There's only Orla here and her partner was killed in the fire.'

Macleod nodded and Ross opened the door fully allowing the party to step inside. Hearing the door lock behind him Macleod dragged Finlay through the kitchen and into a rear room where he let the man collapse to the floor.

'We need to search the house, Ross and then blockade the doors if we can,' suggested Macleod.

'Won't that look obvious, sir. I mean they'll know we're in here then.'

'It might come to a stand until the helicopter gets back.'

'That doesn't sound good, sir. Maybe we should contact the Arnolds on the radio. He might be able to bring the boat around to the harbour and we could get away from there.'

'Are you going to escape?' a voice asked from the dark.

Macleod spun around and he saw a young woman looking at him from the dark of a doorway. She was holding a large kitchen knife and stood in her pyjamas. Her hair was tied back in a plait and there were tears in her eyes.

'We are,' Ross replied. 'You can come, Orla, if you want to. Someone here killed Kiera, even after you sat by her and cared for her. There's something more going on here than you know. They killed Kiera for a reason and they'll kill you too now that the game is up. Put the knife down and we'll take you with us, Orla.'

Macleod watched the woman knowing that any call or shout could bring the parties looking for them to their location.

175

Bracing himself to move quickly to suppress the woman depending on her subsequent actions, he swallowed hard as he watched his colleague try to reason with her.

'She didn't love me. I knew it, but I didn't want to say. It was the drugs they fed her. Keep an eye on her, better than working those drug cesspits he had in Glasgow. And she was something else. You saw Kiera, she was something else. But that boy distracted her.'

'What boy?' asked Ross.

'The Arnold boy. Couldn't stop himself coming over for a look. Even after Mandy was killed. You'd have thought that would have stopped him. He saw it and we thought about putting an end to him but to get rid of a whole family, you'd have to be clever. A random accident on a sparsely populated island. That wouldn't work.'

Orla's eyes seemed to be distant, remembering things that had gone before. Macleod could see Ross edging closer and wondered if he was wise to do so. But the woman could easily call out or even attack so the situation needed contained quickly. The Inspector was regretting his decision to investigate without the helicopter, but that decision had been made and now was no time to be dwelling on the past.

'It's okay,' whispered Ross, 'you can come away with us. The helicopter will come and we can go. We'll let you go far away from here, witness protection. A new life.' He reached forward with his hand and touched Orla's dangling arm. 'Come on, you'll be safe.'

The door of the kitchen opened causing Macleod to spin round and look from the other room. A young woman maybe eighteen or so stood in the doorway in her dressing gown, with pyjamas underneath. The cartoon motif running along the leg seemed surreal in the tension of the moment and the red hair reminded Macleod of his colleague.

Holding a finger up to his mouth, Macleod indicated the woman should be quiet and waved her in. *This must be the mayor's daughter*, thought Macleod, *and she's probably terrified.* Slowly the woman walked forward as Macleod held up his credentials. She would need to know he was a police officer, that with him she could be safe. Step by step, she made her way over to Macleod until she came into the view of the others in the second room.

'Autumn,' said Ross quietly. Macleod didn't turn away from Autumn but heard the yell from Ross. Flicking his head round, he saw the knife descending to Ross, swift and brutal. Autumn let go a wild grunt but Macleod was knocked aside as she ran past him. From his prone position on the floor, Macleod watched the younger woman jump into the fray and there was a brief period of yelling. Then Orla grunted and she gasped as she fell to the floor. As Macleod righted himself and reached for the fallen woman, he saw the knife emanating from her heart.

He turned and saw Ross clutching his arm, blood seeping his shirt. And as he held up a hand, Autumn gave a coarse howl at the top of her voice.

Chapter 20

Stewart sat in front of the computer and yawned. The day had started some time ago and her boss, DS McGrath, had been delayed on the last part of her journey to Inverness by some roadworks. This had given Stewart time to look into the Donoghue estate and in particular at records into what deliveries had been made to the estate for the island. It turned out that the Viscount's staff were keen talkers and one of the main suppliers of equipment to the Viscount was more than happy to talk about deliveries he had made. There were a number of substances, basic core ingredients in many manufacturing items, specifically in small-scale production of premium flavours and additives. However, there were also ingredients used in basic pharmaceuticals. It proved nothing but made Stewart suspicious.

'Kirsten!' shouted a voice from the door.

'Boss. You're just in time, I was about to head back to the lab and speak to Jona about the fish I brought her. But take a look at this.'

Hope McGrath had barely got inside the door and stopped removing her jacket, instead making her way over Stewart's desk. For a few minutes, Stewart ran through her discoveries.

McGrath stood and watched nodding her head on occasion but gave nothing away.

'What do you think?' asked Stewart.

'It's good but it's not strong enough. If we can tie any of the machinery into manufacturing of drugs, we might have a stronger case. Better still if the Inspector finds something. Let's see what Jona has to say before we think any further on this.'

Stewart was a little disappointed and in trademark fashion pushed her glasses back so that Hope would understand but the Sergeant was already on her way out of the door, so Kirsten ran to follow.

'Have you heard from the Inspector?' asked Hope.

'Nothing in the last hour or so. It's not like him. Maybe he's onto something.'

'And not tell us. It's not like he's a glory hunter, Kirsten. He was worried about Ross, insistent that he should go over. That's not like him either unless something is up. I hate it when he has a gut instinct because he's usually right.'

'He did mention about the people on the island, how they seemed to comprise a manufacturing team for drugs.'

Hope smiled grimly. 'Yes, but he also had no proof. I mean you can do that with information, make an answer before you even start to think.'

Kirsten shook her head quickly. 'Not the boss, he starts off very blank in his mind.'

'Hell, Kirsten, I'll not tell him you said that. Backhanded compliment or what?'

'No, it's a good thing. And it's also why he's often right. He lets things just come to him, has a way of assessing from a distance. It's when it gets up close that it's hard to see the

179

wood for the trees. But he does, even then, although it can take time.'

Hope simply nodded and continued to walk. She knew Stewart was a fan of Macleod but there was even an element of hero worship there. Hope had come to appreciate Seoras, learn from him, and even see him as a friend, but there was definitely no worship going on.

'Hope,' cried Jona, as the pair of women entered the laboratory, 'What have you brought me? The chips? A nice salad? After all, Kirsten brings me fish, and rather expensive ones too.'

'What have you found, Jona?'

'Come over here, the pair of you and take a look.' Jona led them to a bench where two fish lay side by side. 'Ostensibly, there is no difference between these fish. Both decent fish, something you'd pay a premium price for if you say it was caught fairly and in an environmental fashion for some dream eco village in the back of nowhere. Nice business model. One that probably works.'

Hope looked perplexed. 'What you're saying that they are selling the fish properly?'

'Some of it, no doubt. But some of it is merely a vehicle to disguise the distinct smell of something. I suspect there were packets of a drug in the shipment that the fish on the left came out of. We manged to find traces of it, a nasty substance known on the streets of Bangkok as Wipeout. Gives massive highs and incredible lows. Not the most stable of substances so you need to move it on quick and use it. That's why it hasn't got to the UK yet. There's no production facilities close enough. Until now it seems.'

'You mean they're producing it on the island,' asked Hope.

'Makes sense,' said Jona. 'After all, you have someone like the Viscount who has the cash to have tried it before or have friends who might have picked it up at expensive parties. I believe it has been flown in once or twice after production. They caught some on a private plane at Gatwick not long ago.'

'And we need to get down to the estate and stop any of the rest of it getting destroyed,' said Hope. 'Although how do we say we found the fish? After all, Kirsten stole it. It didn't come from a proper search.'

'No, it was given to me,' said Stewart.

'He gave you the other one.'

'Really,' muttered Stewart pushing her glasses back up. 'As I recall, I asked for fish and the man said yes. I fancied that one on the left, and he saw me take it. He gave me the one on the right, but he didn't stop me taking the other one, the contaminated one. It was a gift. At least that's how I saw it.'

'Cross contamination,' said Jona, 'horrible thing.'

Hope stared at her colleagues and then decided. 'Stewart, get onto the drug squad and have them meet us at the estate entrance. Give them the location of the fish in case anyone tries to move anything beforehand. Time to catch a load on the premises.'

Nearly three hours later, Hope stood outside the gate to the Donoghue estate, watching colleagues from the drug squad making a move on the warehouse that stored the items from and for the Monach Islands. Stewart was up ahead assisting, having been the only person who had seen inside the estate. Jona Nakamura was waiting for the go ahead with her team to thoroughly search the premises and Hope could see the excitement in her housemate's eyes. Her compact friend never gave much away but she was going to enjoy this one.

But Hope's thoughts were on Macleod. There had been no contact, no word of how he had got on. Nor any word of how Ross was. Alan was such a faithful colleague, Hope wondered how he had been taking the lead. Sometimes she thought Ross would care too much about people. Sometimes you had to make a judgement and just go for it.

The cars waiting at the gates suddenly drove forward onto the estate and Hope followed behind in her car. There was a warehouse and she saw Stewart entering at the front of the cavalcade. Hope could have insisted on being up there too, but it was Kirsten's moment. She had worked hard and deserved a little bit of recognition. Whilst everyone was entering the building, Hope took a call from the Inverness station.

A polite desk Sergeant patched Hope through to a mobile and a pilot called Diggs. The man ran through what was happening on the island and how he had left the Inspector and his two fellow officers on the island as they were looking for Lucy. He was about to return but wanted to make sure the message got to someone who could act based on it.

'Are they okay?' asked Hope.

'As far as I'm aware. As I said, I'm returning for them now. But I think you need to get some proper forces out there and take control of the island. Could also do with getting everyone off the island and somewhere safe. I'm not overly keen to go back myself but your Inspector has kept us safe so far.'

'Can we get in contact with you once you're airborne?' asked Hope.

'You can route comms through the ARCC at the Coastguard but in truth they are having difficulty getting us when we are down low. This is a quick extraction job and then we'll only search from the air, so we stay safe.'

Thanking the man, Hope made her way inside to the warehouse and sought out Stewart. She was briefing a senior drugs officer on the containers she had previously found and where the fish with the drugs on it had come from. Quick samples were being taken and Jona was busy securing the site forensically.

'Excuse me, Inspector,' said Hope putting herself between a large man with dark hair and Stewart, 'if I can have my colleague back soon—as it's rather urgent.'

'Of course, Sergeant, I think we can take this from here. And it's Glen, not Inspector. Less formality, that's the rule.'

'Indeed, Hope. Hope McGrath.'

The man nodded his head and shook Hope's hand firmly. 'Oh, I know who you are. Whole station knows your unit. Pass my regards onto Inspector Macleod.'

'Seoras, Glen, in the spirit of it and all that.' *Seoras will hate that,* thought Hope, *but I'll drag him into the new century if I have to haul him there.*

Hope took Stewart to one side and briefed her on what had been said by the pilot. 'We need to get some reinforcements organised as by the sound of it, the place has gone crazy. Lucy is also missing but don't tell Jona at the moment. There's nothing she can do and she's busy. I think the best bet might be to find a military vessel nearby that could assist. The winds are still high so I don't know if the police helo will fly. And we need numbers. Of all the places to pick, why out there, Stewart?'

'Okay, I'm going into the rear of the car, and I'll get on the laptop and get some numbers for coordinating a response. But you'll need to start talking up the chain, Hope. We're going to need to have some clout if they want us to effectively storm an island.'

Hope held up her hands. 'Stewart, they are asking for help, not some D-Day landing party. But we'll need armed response as there's killers there. Get me those numbers and I'll talk with the DCI. I just pray they can stay safe until the cavalry comes. Let's get cracking.'

Hope called the DCI and after a brief conversation, the woman said she would get things moving, especially as one of their own was missing. Stood in the cold outside an estate in the mountains, Hope was grateful that the DCI was taking everything on board. The only instruction she gave Hope was to find Donoghue, the only missing piece of the puzzle.

Hope made her way to the main office where a tall man was answering questions about shipments and deliveries from the Monach islands to a Sergeant for the drugs squad. It was clear to Hope that this man was the representative for Donoghue, given that he was answering all the questions and he was also denying everything. Excuses such as drugs dumped at sea, to shipments being spiked unknowingly were being floated as the truth but the Sergeant was having none of it.

'Darren, isn't it?' asked Hope. 'Sorry, can I butt in for a minute? Hope McGrath. I need to ask this man some questions.'

'Sure thing, Hope, and I do recognise you.'

'Sorry, Darren, what's his name?'

'My name is Arthur Finchley and if you don't know my name then I can hardly be the one you are looking for. I have told this dullard of a police officer that we on the estate have had nothing to do with the situation. It has clearly been put upon us and we are victims, I tell you, victims, of a deep fraud, and—'

'Arthur, shut up,' said Hope and saw Darren grin. 'I have a

situation out on that island, a rather deadly one. I need to know where your boss is and fast. If not, I will throw the book at you for obstruction and if any more people die then I will hold you accountable for those deaths and charge you as an accessory. Do you understand? Where is Viscount Donoghue?'

'People dead, you say. On the island. Not just Mandy Novak?'

'No, Mr Finchley, not just Mandy Novak. Things have taken a profoundly serious turn and we will be looking for anyone. We also have one of our own missing, and one dead. There's a world of pain coming, and the Viscount is at the centre of it. Tell me where he is, or you can happily join him in that pain.'

'Look, can we have a word away from other ears?'

Hope nodded and Darren, recognising the request, walked away for a moment.

'I believe he's meeting someone tonight. He had negotiated a deal with a player. You can probably bag them too but just keep me out of it. I can take the rap for bluffing here, do you hear, but I'm not taking any rap for killings. I can wait out a short jail term as a man just doing what he was told but I'm not going inside for a long time. Donoghue has enemies, do you hear, enemies. I doubt I'd last long. So, promise me, I'll be tagged only to this and nothing else.'

Hope shook her head. 'I can't promise anything and as it's just you and me, you'll have to trust me anyway, as there's no witnesses. Tell me what you know, and I'll see what I can do.'

Arthur Finchley seemed to consider his options for a minute, which Hope found interesting as she was not that sure he had any. Then he waved her in close.

'The Braemar duck pond.'

Hope took a long hard stare at the man. 'Is that a joke?'

'No, it's off the beaten track and away from watching eyes. Also, not somewhere people tend to go in the snow. And it's also neutral territory because it's going to be just them. No one else.'

'When you say just them, I take it this other guy's a big player.'

Arthur Finchley nodded and smiled. 'Yes, very. Donoghue was looking at expanding the operation but was surprised when he got a call from this man. There were a number he could have worked through, but he always thought this man was an enemy. But the chance was too good to turn down.

'And who is it?'

'The king of the East side trade. And if I tell you, you have to never breathe a word how you found out.'

'Okay, who is it?'

'John Bonnar.'

Oh hell, thought Hope. 'When? When is it?'

'Half an hour.'

Hope raced past a surprised Sergeant Darren who looked back at Arthur Finchley. 'What the hell did you just say to her?'

'Nothing,' replied Finchley, as cool as anything, 'she's just a touch behind schedule.'

Chapter 21

'There's nothing,' said Macleod. 'She's gone.' He stared down at the body of Orla McIlroy and saw the anguish still on her face. 'It's okay, Ross, self-defence. How's your arm?'

'But I didn't kill her. I didn't.' The constable's face was white and clutched his arm as the blood seeped through to his jacket. Macleod looked around the kitchen and found a towel, bringing it to Ross and wrapping it tight around his wound. The Inspector tried to give a cheery smile which was no doubt completely inappropriate, but he needed to keep his man focused.

'It's okay Ross, you did okay, she was wild. And you protected Autumn.'

Autumn was hanging on the back of Ross's jacket and she was crying, sobbing into his neck. Death, especially a brutal death, affected everyone differently, but he was worried about his Constable. The denials he was coming out with were perfectly normal but there was something else in the way he said it.

But there was no time to get deeply into Ross's reaction. Autumn had let go such a loud howl when Orla had died that Macleod was sure everyone would be coming for them. He glanced at Finlay sitting on his bottom in the kitchen. The blow to his head had left the man so groggy, Macleod wanted to tuck him into a bed and let him sleep for a year. But they needed to get on the move again. Rushing to the kitchen window, Macleod looked into the night but saw no one in the snow. The moon, crisp and bright, like one borrowed from a Christmas film, was lighting up the immediate surroundings.

'We'll need to get away and find another hiding hole,' advised Macleod. 'Can you stand, Ross? Looks like you've lost a fair amount of blood.'

Ross pulled himself unsteadily to his feet, shrugging off Autumn in the process. The young woman then grabbed his hand, looking up at him with eyes full of tears.

'I can walk, sir, but maybe not too far,' said Ross.

'In the circumstances, I think you can call me, Seoras.' Macleod saw the grin on Ross's face and knew he had brought a lift to the man. It was a silly joke, but he needed Ross in a mood that while not good, would at least be alert.

'Let's get everyone to a new place to hide and I'll see if I can find something better,' Macleod said and ushered Ross and Autumn into the kitchen. He then hauled Finlay to his feet. The officer was not heavy and with an arm around Macleod, he staggered along. Opening the rear door, Macleod looked here and there before setting out around the rear of the house with Finlay. Slowly they crept along until coming to the end of the house and Macleod peered around the corner in search of any movement. There was none but his heart was thumping. One wrong move and they could all be dead.

But something was bothering him. Where was the entourage running to the scream? They had been pursued from the underground silo; he was sure of it. But why was everyone not being raised up to come after them. After all, just how secret were the underground rooms? You couldn't keep that sort of thing a secret, could you? Was everyone in on this? Autumn was but a child really, a teenager so maybe she was brought here by her father. But she would have seen things. She would be in danger.

Amanda Novak had obviously seen too much or maybe there had been disagreements. But why fake a suicide? In a lot of ways, it seemed inept. Macleod's mind raced as his eyes scanned and he could feel himself sweating despite the extreme cold. And then he saw something in the snow.

The dark image in the snow was some fifty feet away but Macleod had an idea what it was. He had seen too many slumped bodies in his time, those who had collapsed like a bag of potatoes when they had been struck down. Turning around and holding up a hand, urging the others to wait, Macleod stole over in the snow and came face to face with a mop of hair in the white. Gently pulling the head back, he saw lifeless eyes and then quickly checked for a pulse. There was nothing. But he recognised the woman who had attacked him in the silo. She smelt of fish too—in fact, reeked of it.

But Macleod was not trying to protect himself from another whiff of the foul-smelling clothes. Instead, he rifled along looking for a wound, something that would show a cause of death. As he ran a hand past her chest, he felt the delicate hole in her top. His hand touched the blood around her heart.

Someone had a gun, and not just any gun. This was so close to where they had been hiding it must have been used with a silencer. But who? *Come on, Seoras, think.* Turning back to his colleagues, he held up a hand again and now ran to the rear of the next house. From the corner he stared out into the

189

settlement's square. There was a figure there too. It was too open to run over and examine it but someone else was dead. What was happening? A kill order? A clearing up of everyone who could talk about what was happening?

'This is Coastguard helicopter, channel zero. Are you there, Inspector?'

Finlay was holding the radio, but Macleod could hear every word clearly. Running back over to his colleagues, he grabbed it and quickly turned down the volume.

'Coastguard? Inspector Macleod. We are at the main settlement, and the situation is precarious. We have had engagement with hostiles and are currently hiding out. Suggest you do not come directly above us as you may be shot at.'

'Roger, Inspector. Give us a minute.'

Macleod wondered what Captain Diggs would do. By rights with hostile action taking place, he should not engage and simply call in someone more equipped, like a navy helicopter. But that would take time, and this was probably an ex-military man. Maybe he could come up with an option.

Autumn was still clinging to Ross and he now had the girl's head on his good shoulder. She seemed extremely attached to him and had even raced to his rescue. It had been foolish, but Ross had managed to succumb Orla McIlroy, even if the action taken had been fatal. If Macleod could simply get his team off the island that would be enough now. Except where was Lucy?

'Inspector, Coastguard helicopter.'

'I'm here,' said Macleod hoarsely into the radio.

'We can see several heat signatures in your area; however, none seem to be moving. There's one behind the house I think your sheltering in. The first one up from the east.'

'That's where we are.'

'Well, we can see you, but we are quite high up. There's someone in the ten o'clock from the rear of the house. And there's someone in the square.'

'Understood. The one at the rear is dead, and the other I think is deceased also.' Macleod kept his scan of the surroundings going while he spoke.

'Well, we can also see that most houses are occupied, several figures but none moving.'

Bizarre, thought Macleod, *unless they are hiding, not part of the clear up. Innocents.* He'd need to go get them. One might be Lucy.

'If we accept them as hostile where can you pick us up?'

'I suggest that you head over to the hall and run from there toward the spit that has the beach beside it, on the south, near the harbour. We'll route in low from the sea and keep ourselves out of range of an attack. When we see you running for the spit, we'll move in. It'll be a quick hover just above the ground, doors open and in. No hanging around Inspector, we'll be a sitting duck while you get on board.'

Macleod wondered if he should tell the man to simply get some reinforcements but the danger to him and his people was too great. Maybe they could get to the spit as they had stayed hidden so far. And there was that thought again that something was not right.

'Ross, I want you to take Finlay and Autumn here to the rear of the hall. I'll be over shortly. From there we're going to rendezvous with the helicopter and get out of here. I'm going to do a quick search for Lucy first of all. There's a number of images in those houses.'

'Sir, not alone. Let me come with you,' said Ross.

'You're in no condition Constable, and neither is Finlay, he's still away with the fairies after that blow. No, you get Autumn and Finlay to the hut, and here, take the radio. If I'm not there in five, call the helicopter for a run to the spit. And then get on board.'

'I can't let you—'

'As your senior officer, I am instructing you in what to do. Follow those instructions, Ross. Am I clear?'

'Yes, sir.' It was almost like Ross had sworn at him, and Macleod saw the anger on the man's face.

'Alan,' Macleod whispered, 'trust me.'

There was a nod, simple and brief but it conveyed the world to Macleod. As he watched his colleague gather the small group and make off into the night, Macleod steeled himself for a deadly game of cat and mouse. Who was killing these people and where were they? Which house held the danger? He had about five minutes and then he needed to get going, so Macleod refused to hang about but instead made his way along the rear of the house and across the gap to the next one. His heart was in his mouth as he ran the gap but there was no sound. But then there would hardly be one, would there, if they had a silencer.

Opening the rear of the house, he tore through the kitchen. Looking here and there before making his way into the front room. An old man was slumped in a chair. Alfie Collins had a bullet hole through his forehead. Macleod glanced around the rest of the room but there was nothing, no person in the shadows about to execute him as well. The room was a blur as he exited into a hallway. Climbing the stairs, he tried to tread on the side of the steps, to make them creak less but when one squeaked, he simply legged it as fast as he could onto the landing.

He opened the first bedroom door crouching at knee height so as not to present a target. Slipping into the room, he saw a double bed and a woman lying on it. On her pillow was the blood from a shot to the temple. Probably killed in her sleep. Not that much comfort could be taken from it. The woman was old, and Macleod thought about those who were on the island. This was Alfie and Edna Collins, the chemical engineer and the pharmacist. They would have known what was happening in the silo. They would have been at the thick of it. Not anymore.

Macleod quickly checked the remaining bedrooms but there was nothing, no sign of disturbance at all. The bathroom was the same so Macleod stole a glance from the bedroom window at the square. He could see the dead body in the snow but there was nothing else. When he exited the house and stole around to the next one, Macleod realised he would never cover the rest of the houses in time. But Lucy was somewhere, and he would give her every chance he could.

The next house had its back door lying open. Macleod saw a skirt blowing in the wind and as he approached, he thought the figure to be that of a strong woman, larger than average. Creeping up to the side of the door, he peered inside and saw a man on the floor. Quickly he inspected the bodies. The woman had a wound to her chest on the right side. She also had two shots to the head. The man simply had a large chunk of his cranium separated.

There was no time for wonder or condolences; he had a colleague to find. Macleod tore through the house like a wild man. Something in his mind was telling him, he would be fine because there was no danger. But the other side of him trembled at every pause he made. At every corner, his heart beat fast, knowing he could be jumping out to a loaded gun. Sometimes you had to do and not think.

The last house would be the Mayor's. Again, he came in by the rear door and thanked the Lord that these islanders left all their doors open. Everything about the house was still and Macleod crept through the kitchen. There was a dining room off it and the table was still set for dinner. When he found the living room, the television was playing a DVD, but the volume was off.

In the hall, Macleod found Mayor Duncan Forester. That was everyone, so it must have been the Arnold boy. But there was the burnt body that still had no identification. Or maybe it was David Arnold realising that his son had paid a price. Or was there someone else hidden on the island they did not know about. Or was it . . . ?

How could Macleod have been so stupid not to see it? She had jumped into the fray. Ross had told him, hadn't he? And then came a sound from upstairs. Macleod froze as he heard the scratching. Then came a thump. Someone was in the house. Carefully, Macleod stepped over the body of Duncan Forester and made his way up the stairs, this time going a lot slower than before. In his head, he had always believed the previous houses would be empty. In fact, he had believed the same about this one. But it was not.

At the landing he crept along, hands ready to grab anyone coming into view. Slowly he pushed open the main bedroom door. Nothing moved but he heard the scratching sound again. Spinning in the landing, he opened another door and saw a teenager's bedroom. Slowly he peered in, but it was empty. A number of fluffy animals lined the bed and he saw pictures of boy bands on the wall. This was the bedroom of Autumn Forester, and it was brilliantly done. Everything about her was.

Behind him came a muffled cry. Quickly Macleod threw open the door behind him and found the bathroom. It was empty and so he tried the last door on the landing, gingerly pushing it away from him. In the dark on the floor was a woman. She had tape across her mouth and was strapped to a chair which she had managed to topple. But her legs and hands were still bound to it. Macleod pulled back the tape.

'Get me out of here,' said the woman and as Macleod untied her, he recognised her from the laboratory. In fact, Jona had mentioned her. Yes, this was Lucy.

'There's a helicopter coming, down by the strip near the harbour. We need to go. Can you run?'

Lucy looked at Macleod as if he were stupid. 'I'm standing; I think I can run.'

'Good,' said Macleod, caught a little off guard by the attitude. 'And there's a killer out there, armed I reckon. I think it's Autumn Forester.'

'Well, yeah,' said Lucy, as if the statement was obvious.

'How do you know?'

'I heard her shoot her Dad.'

'So why are you still here?' asked Macleod, pushing Lucy out of the bedroom door.

'Because he was waiting for someone to tell him what to do with me. Never told his daughter. I don't think he knew about her. Communications are out, hadn't you noticed?'

'Yes, Lucy, yes I had. But Autumn's now making for the helicopter with Ross and Finlay. We need to catch that flight.'

'Then we'd better run. Come on,' said Lucy tearing off down

195

the stairs. 'Bit of a stupid move to leave her with your guys.'

Like I don't realise that now, thought Macleod, racing off behind Lucy.

Chapter 22

Hope jumped into the driver's seat, catching Stewart unaware in the rear. As the car drove off, Kirsten fell sideways with her laptop sliding off her lap on top of her. Righting herself and her glasses, Kirsten stared at her boss and colleague wondering if she had lost her mind.

'What the hell's up? Someone die?'

'Not yet, but there's time,' said Hope, accelerating hard through the estate and then exiting to the main road.

'A little word from the wise? What's happening?'

'Bonnar is meeting Donoghue and I reckon he means to kill him. They're meant to be getting into cahoots with the drugs but it's a ruse to get Donoghue. I'm sure of it. The word's out about Mandy Novak and Bonnar's not going to be happy given your run-in with him. I think Mandy was quite something to Bonnar. And I don't think Donoghue even knows who she was. Just someone to use on his drug island.'

Kirsten climbed into the front of the car, a feat made all the more difficult by how Hope was throwing the car along the mountain roads. The snow had been cleared in the main but with the chill in the area, Kirsten wondered if black ice would form. She could not tell if the roads had been gritted but Hope was certainly treating them like they were.

Snow was falling again, and Hope thought that even drug dealers must be mad to meet to do deals on a night like this. She would rather be in with Jona watching one of those stupid Romcom films she liked. In fact, she would rather be inside doing a jigsaw if it came to it. Heck, they drove her mad. But her mind returned to the road as the stone fences and wooden gates passed her by on the side of the road and lit up for just a moment by the car headlights.

'Can't be far to Braemar,' said Hope with just an intonation that said Stewart should find out.

'Did he say where in Braemar?'

'The duck pond.'

'Seriously. The duck pond? Is that a big thing in Braemar? Or is that a cover for something else?'

'Just take a look and see if there's a damn duck pond, Kirsten. And then give me directions when we get there.'

When Braemar did arrive, Hope saw the houses, lights peering out through the dark behind tall trees and neat stone fences. Everything was clean and tidy and she felt bad driving at speed through the town.

'Left,' shouted Stewart and Hope swung the car in front of a motorist waving a fist. The blue lights would make the job easier but would also scatter the very people she was trying to get close to.

'Right!'

'A bit more warning would help,' shouted Hope to her colleague.

'It's these damn screens. Left again.'

'Okay, but I don't want to go round in circles and arrive late.'

'Straight on, it's down this street right towards the bottom.'

The road became narrow and Hope slowed the car down. As

she passed houses that sat closer to the road there were no pavements and a general more rustic feel rather than a grand highland theme was the order of the day.

'That's it, just ahead.'

Hope pulled the car over, parking as best she could to one side of the road. Quietly they exited the vehicle and walked briskly along the roadside. The moon was clouded over as the snow continued to fall. It was to last the night and then bring in clearer skies, skies that Macleod would already be seeing.

'There's a car park up ahead,' said Stewart, pointing it out. 'I think they can walk over to the duck pond; at least, that's what it looked like on the map. Do you want me to circle round, cut through the back of a house?'

'Good idea, we could do with picking them both up. But be careful, I reckon Bonnar is here to kill Donoghue. I'll route in from the road through the car park and take them from the other side.'

Hope zipped up her leather jacket and shivered in the bitter weather. Jobs in the summer were always better. As she made her way slowly into the car park, she saw two cars. *It must be them; after all, do people watch ducks in the dark? Do ducks come out at night? Don't they have little houses or something? Jona was the one for that sort of information.*

And then Hope saw two shadows beyond the duck pond. They were a distance away, but she could hear the start of an argument.

'I thought you were here for business. I told you there's going to be a delay until I get the second unit up and running but then you'll have enough Wipeout to make you a packet. There's no need to get cross. It's just a setback. And there's plenty more junkies where they came from.'

Hope watched as the man who had not been talking threw a punch at the other man. The talker fell backwards and then scrambled away. But then he produced something and pointed it at his assailant.

'That's not business. That's not how we do things. Anyway, what's a junkie to you?'

'You made her a junkie! You stole her from me then took her away to that Godforsaken place. What else would she do out there except get stoned and slowly die? She bloody well killed herself in your care, you idiot. She was mine!'

'I think not,' said the gun holder. 'If I remember correctly, she was long gone from you when she started taking my drugs. Volunteer to the cause, quite a spritely girl with it too. Now see sense and see her for the drugged-up tart that she was. We have good business to do, business that will make us both a lot of money. You don't want to throw it away on some dead whore.'

Hope crept further forward but she saw the angry man reach for the gun holder only to step back as the weapon was placed into his face.

'It's unfortunate but she'd have been dead anyway. I've given the order to mop up. My silent party will sort it all out so I can start somewhere else. It's my business and sure I'll have to go somewhere hotter that this crappy backwater, but you know, I think I'm going to like it. You can get in on it, Bonnar, but you need to see sense, man.'

Hope was now about fifty yards away and wary of getting any closer. She scanned the terrain, trying to spot Stewart but the woman was nowhere in sight. How were they going to get a jump on these men?

'Do you know what, Bonnar? I don't think you want my

business, and as you know about it, that means you're a risk. You should have got your gun out quicker. Now you'll pay for that.'

Hope saw the man line the gun up on Bonnar, making sure the shot would not miss. It was only a two-second pause, but it was then she saw a figure jump out from the dark. Hope reckoned it was a bin of some sort, but it had been shielding Stewart from sight and she now took down the man with the gun forcing him to the ground.

Hope ran forward, shouting at Bonnar to lie down on the ground. 'Police, get down, now.' Bonnar put his hands up and slowly lay down on the ground and placed his hands behind his back.

'Have you got him, Stewart?'

'Yes Sergeant, he's going nowhere.' As Stewart pulled the man to his feet, Hope almost laughed at the size difference. Kirsten packed a punch, but she always looked like some sort of champion mouse bringing in the big cat.

'Let's see if you boys can behave. Or do I need to get us a van to bring you in.'

'I don't think we'll both be going into the station,' said Bonnar.

'What makes you think so, Bonnar? I heard the discussion. You're implicated and I need you for further questioning. It'll be two cosy jail cells for the pair of you.'

'Don't worry,' said Bonnar, 'I've brought my pyjamas. Doubt Donoghue will need any.'

'I think I can speak-' started Donoghue but a loud crack filled the air.

Hope saw Stewart fall to the ground but not before Donoghue's head was whipped back. He fell with Stewart making a vain attempt to catch him. Hope dropped to the ground, shaking, knowing she was exposed, the large flat area around the duck pond giving no cover. There were cries from the ducks in their houses for the night and other wildlife scattered. But Bonnar stood motionless.

'It's fine, you can get up. I think it came from about a mile away, maybe closer, I don't know how good these people are with their guns. But they had a long time getting good.'

Hope looked up and then crawled over to Stewart who was face down but staring at the severely damaged head of Viscount Donoghue. The man was clearly dead. 'You hurt, Kirsten.'

'No, but he isn't coming back.'

Hope began to stand up and walked back to Bonnar. 'You knew, didn't you? You damn well knew where your hitman would be.'

'My hitman? That had nothing to do with me. Not my fault if the Irish boys followed me. Maybe they had a gripe with the good Viscount. Though, I think that score is settled now.'

Hope looked up at the surrounding hills and could see extraordinarily little. There was snow everywhere and maybe the person was in white. If Bonnar was right, and she had no way to disbelieve him, Mr Flaherty had called off Helen Lilly because he had found things out another way. His daughter must have been on the island. Maybe she had been the girl in the fire.

'Did you hear what he said, boss?'

'What, Kirsten?'

'Donoghue said he had someone on the island, there to clean up. We need to warn the Inspector.'

Hope nodded at Stewart and pointed to the car back on the road. As she rang into the station to request help for the crime scene and to see about blocking off a five-mile perimeter, Hope heard her colleague in the background.

'I really should thank you,' said Bonnar, 'you may have saved my life. Was always a risk coming here without a gun because you never can tell how people will be. Especially their mad fantasy ideas about what I do at nights. I'm a successful businessman. After all, you've seen my hotel.'

'Shut up!' There was a small cry from Bonnar, but she could tell how Stewart had hurt him. And she did not want to know. But she heard him cry out again.

Chapter 23

'Come on, Inspector. You said five minutes and it's been five minutes. They won't wait; you said so.'

Macleod was ready to kill his newly found colleague. For the entire run from the houses to the strip where the helicopter would find them, Lucy had constantly gone on about how slow he was and how she would miss the helicopter if she stayed with him. His puffing from the run made any reply impossible and his legs were screaming at him. The snow, thick and heavy from the last few days fall, was sapping the strength, not that he had been given the chance to refresh already-failing legs.

Ahead of him, Macleod could see a small band of people. One was waving his hand at them. It was Ross. God bless you, Ross, God bless you. Although the wind was still giving a stiff counter to his stride, Macleod could hear a rumbling in the air. Beyond Ross was the sea, crashing and as cold as it came. But he saw a glorious sight rise from below the cliff edge and a red light flashed in the night. There was also a white one on the rear of the aircraft. Macleod thought there was another but maybe it was because the aircraft was side on to them, setting down a short distance from Ross's group.

True to his word, Captain Diggs was keeping the aircraft just off the ground and Macleod saw Dave the paramedic assisting Ross, Finlay and Autumn into the helicopter. Turning back, he waved at Macleod, encouraging him on.

Now that he had his goal in sight, Macleod wondered how best to handle this. He couldn't just blurt out the woman had a gun. She might have everyone dead by the time he could react. And where was her weapon concealed?

Dave assisted the Inspector into the aircraft, and he was thrown into a seat. Lucy came in behind him and he saw her sit down but her eyes were on Autumn. Macleod understood Lucy had a form of autism but really did she have no idea she was giving the game away. If she kept this up, Macleod would have to react sooner rather than later. His eyes shot to Autumn and he watched her sit down in her seat and start to buckle up. What would her plan be? Would she take over the aircraft? Would she wait it out and make a run for it on landing?

Lucy was still watching her, and Macleod reckoned that Autumn was aware of it. Part of him could not believe this teenager was capable of such murder as he had seen in the houses, but Macleod would not underestimate her in any sense. Macleod placed his straps over him and connected the buckle which Dave checked. The helicopter was already speeding away from the island, a short trip to Benbecula to regroup. But as Dave checked seat belts, he saw that Autumn had no intention of fastening hers. The woman slipped her arms back out and Macleod saw her reach inside her jumper.

Unclipping his belt, Macleod raced across the cabin just as Autumn pulled out the handgun complete with silencer. Dave, unaware of the danger tried to push Macleod back into his seat and was roundly shoved aside. As Autumn made for the gap which led through to the pilots in the cockpit, Macleod reached for her from behind, placing his hands upon her wrist. But she was deceptively strong, and they twisted around, falling back into the cabin. A shot went off, making a dull sound, quite unimpressive. There was a cry, but Macleod still had a hand on Autumn's wrist. She twisted the gun, attempting to fire at Lucy but Macleod managed to force the weapon to one side and a tear appeared in the seat beside Lucy's head. She screamed and Macleod felt Dave jump on top of Autumn and himself.

'Hit her man, get the gun out of her hand.' Macleod was struggling to maintain a grip on the woman, but Dave threw a punch to her head and the gun fell out of her hand. Macleod could hear the Captain screaming, demanding to know what was going on. A moment later the co-pilot was through and jumping on top of Autumn.

'Secure the gun, Lucy,' Macleod shouted at the forensic officer and was almost surprised when she made her way over to the weapon and picked it up. Without hesitation she pointed it at Autumn.

'Don't move, I'll fire. I will shoot you.'

Macleod managed to get Autumn's arms behind her and looked for his handcuffs but there were none there. 'Ross, do you have cuffs?' There was no answer. Macleod watched Finlay stand from his seat and grab his cuffs and throw them at Macleod. Then he turned and stared at one of the seats Macleod struggled to see. 'Ross, you there?'

Snapping the cuffs on Autumn's wrists, Macleod watched Finlay look with horror in the direction of Ross. Macleod's heart sank. 'No! No, no, no!' Getting to his feet he saw the blood at Ross's neck and heard the rasp coming from his throat.

Macleod was numb, his eyes starting to swell with tears, but Dave rushed forward. 'Digsy, we need to go, nearest hospital.' The paramedic then raced off details, medical terminology that made no sense to Macleod. But what did make sense was that Ross's eyes were closed and blood was pouring from his neck.

Macleod felt useless. Dave's colleague, the winch operator, and Lucy assisted the paramedic as Macleod saw something being placed inside Ross's throat. Finlay came over to Macleod and they secured Autumn on the floor. From the conversations happening around him, Macleod understood they were heading for Raigmore Hospital in Inverness. For most of the flight, Macleod looked at the back of Autumn's head, forcing himself to not imagine placing blow after blow into the rear of it. And he would look up through blurred eyes to see Ross, his neck now packed.

When they landed on the helipad at Raigmore, a team of medical staff assisted Dave and the winch operator to get Ross onto a trolley. Without looking back, they tore off into the hospital. Macleod waited for a police detail to arrive and then handed over Autumn. Making his way into the hospital, he found the men's toilets, entered a cubicle, and began throwing up. *Not Ross, dear God, not Ross.*

* * *

'Is the boss okay?'

'No, Kirsten, he's hardly said a word. Doubt he will until Ross comes out of surgery.' Hope looked through the glass to the room inside where Macleod sat with Ross's partner.

207

'Were they hopeful?'

'I don't know, they just took him in. No one's heard anything since.'

'So, she just killed them all before leaving, even her father?'

'Apparently it's not her father. She's been dumping all the blame on Donoghue, but I don't think she's realised he's dead yet. Said he gave the kill order.'

Stewart nodded and looked through the window at Macleod. Then something triggered with her. 'How? All the communications were down.'

'Satellite phone. They had power but no comms. She had a satellite phone stashed away. We're waiting for that to be confirmed by the team going to the island. There's no one out there now. Even the Arnolds came off the island once they realised their boy was truly missing. It's not a definite but my guess is he was seeing Kiera Harris behind everyone's back. Lucy said that Orla and Kiera were close, essentially a couple in the narrative of the island but it seems Kiera Harris, or Mary Flaherty was actually more into the drugs Orla provided.'

'Was she a test subject for Wipeout?'

Hope shrugged her shoulders and curled her mouth up. 'It's not that clear cut. Orla recruited her in Glasgow. At least I reckon she was the mysterious person Helen Lilly had been tracking. But Lucy said Orla was properly cut up about Kiera, watched over her.'

'Did the Arnolds know anything about their son being involved?' asked Stewart. 'The boy must have been lonely. Twenty-year-old males have too much testosterone running around to be in isolation with their family. Makes sense he would seek company.'

'We can't say what the exact relationship was, but it got him killed.'

The door to the relatives' waiting room opened and Macleod stumbled out. He looked weary, his eyes red and full of concern.

'No news,' he said. 'Still in there. Kirsten, go and sit in there for ten minutes; I really need a break.'

There was no hesitation from Stewart and she gave a quick comforting smile before leaving her boss. Hope reached forward and simply hugged Seoras.

'Not your fault. She could have killed anyone with a random shot. You managed to stop her taking the helicopter down. And you got lucky, having a paramedic right there. He'll come through. He has to.'

Macleod nodded. 'Times like these I wished I smoked or drank or something.'

'I imagined you praying—that sounds more your thing.'

'I haven't stopped. I've begged Him. But He doesn't say anything. You have to just trust, just believe. There's nothing else.'

'Come on, let's get some air.'

They walked in silence along the fresh corridors, recently scrubbed by a cleaning crew, before descending the stairs to the bottom of the hospital block. Once outside, Hope felt the chill in the air and wrapped her leather jacket around her.

'Are you okay, Hope? They just shot him right in front of you. Doesn't matter if it's scum like Donoghue, it's still a shock.'

'I've taken a leaf from your book, just going on, immersing myself in the case. But I doubt we'll catch the gunman. Might have been a paid job rather than an Irish friend. The hard bit is tying anything to Bonnar despite David Arnold admitting being in his pay. A watching brief. Must have been good money to take your family there.'

'Skint fisherman, must have sounded like a dream. But he paid for it, lost a son, Hope. Clever of Bonnar though, knowing a rival was up to something.'

'I think it was more for a watching brief on Amanda. Bonnar was nowhere near over her. But he was shrewd, even when he dealt with Kirsten. But she did good, really coming along. Her and Ross make a great double act.' Hope sniffed as she said the words. She felt Macleod wrap his arms around her and she began to cry on his shoulder. 'Not Alan, he was the best of us.'

'Still is, Hope. Don't give up.'

For a moment they stood, wrapped up and sniffing on each other's shoulders. People walked past, as they so often do in hospitals, weaving a path that stays just far enough away from someone else's grief. Maybe they had enough of their own.

'I'm going to go up and see Kirsten. After that I need to go and do something. Truth is the help the DCI sent us to wrap things up can handle it all. I just want to do something.'

Macleod nodded and as Hope walked away, she heard him shout her name. 'Hope. I can't do this anymore. I need out. I was so bloody useless watching him fight for breath. He waited for me, did I say? Wouldn't leave me behind.'

'Like I said, Seoras, the best of us.'

Turning back to the door, Hope saw a grinning Stewart running towards her. 'He's out. They said he's going to make it. Lot of work and recovery but he's going to make it. Thank God!'

Hope threw her arms around Stewart and the pair embraced. Then opening her arms, Hope called Seoras over and the three embraced. When the shock of his recovery had sunk in, Macleod told Stewart to get back up and be there for Ross's partner.

'I'll be up in a moment. I just need to give thanks, Kirsten. I'm coming.'

Hope watched Stewart bound away and began to walk after her. But then she stopped. Macleod had his head bowed and she watched his lips move as he silently spoke to his God. She was surprised when two minutes later Macleod was still praying. But rather than disturb him, Hope watched. It was a very personal side to her boss and to see it up close was a privilege. When he opened his eyes, she saw the surprise at her still being there.

'You must have been very grateful,' she said. 'I am, too, if you're speaking to Him again.'

'Most of that wasn't for Ross. I need out, Hope. God knows I need out.'

Read on to discover the Patrick Smythe series!

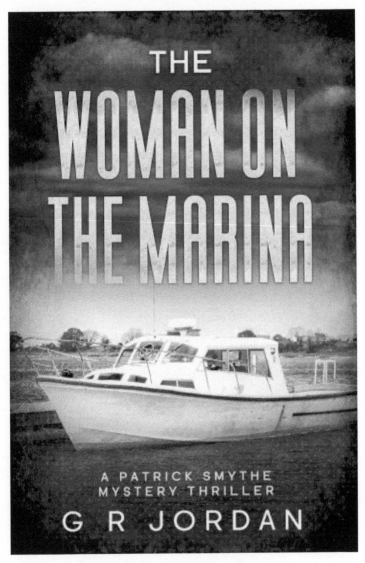

THE
WOMAN ON THE MARINA

A PATRICK SMYTHE
MYSTERY THRILLER

G R JORDAN

Start your Patrick Smythe journey here!

Patrick Smythe is a former Northern Irish policeman who

after suffering an amputation after a bomb blast, takes to the sea between the west coast of Scotland and his homeland to ply his trade as a private investigator. Join Paddy as he tries to work to his own ethics while knowing how to bend the rules he once enforced. Working from his beloved motorboat 'Craigantlet', Paddy decides to rescue a drug mule in this short story from the pen of G R Jordan.

Join G R Jordan's monthly newsletter about forthcoming releases and special writings for his tribe of avid readers and then receive your free Patrick Smythe short story.

Go to https://bit.ly/PatrickSmythe for your Patrick Smythe journey to start!

About the Author

GR Jordan is a self-published author who finally decided at forty that in order to have an enjoyable lifestyle, his creative beast within would have to be unleashed. His books mirror that conflict in life where acts of decency contend with self-promotion, goodness stares in horror at evil, and kindness blindsides us when we at our worst. Corrupting our world with his parade of wondrous and horrific characters, he highlights everyday tensions with fresh eyes whilst taking his methodical, intelligent mainstays on a roller-coaster ride of dilemmas, all the while suffering the banter of their provocative sidekicks.

A graduate of Loughborough University where he masqueraded as a chemical engineer but ultimately played American football, Gary had worked at changing the shape of cereal flakes and pulled a pallet truck for a living. Watching vegetables freeze at -40'C was another career highlight and he was also one of the Scottish Highlands "blind" air traffic controllers.

These days he has graduated to answering a telephone to people in trouble before telephoning other people to sort it out.

Having flirted with most places in the UK, he is now based in the Isle of Lewis in Scotland where his free time is spent between raising a young family with his wife, writing, figuring out how to work a loom and caring for a small flock of chickens. Luckily, his writing is influenced by his varied work and life experience as the chickens have not been the poetical inspiration he had hoped for!

You can connect with me on:
🌐 https://grjordan.com
⬛ https://facebook.com/carpetlessleprechaun

Subscribe to my newsletter:
✉ https://bit.ly/PatrickSmythe

Also by G R Jordan

G R Jordan writes across multiple genres including crime, dark and action adventure fantasy, feel good fantasy, mystery thriller and horror fantasy. Below is a selection of his work. Whilst all books are available across online stores, signed copies are available at his personal shop.

The Satchel (Highlands & Islands Detective Book 11)
A bag is found hanging on a lonely tree in an Inverness park. Inside, a morbid collection of fists tell a tale of murder and intrigue. Can Macleod find the killer and stop a second show of hands?

Battle-weary Macleod must seek to understand a murderer's obsession when a bag of appendages turns up in a local park. But as the links between the victims become more apparent, the possible identities of the killer increases. Can Macleod sift the wheat from the chaff and stop the killer before another bag is full?

Don't raise your hand if you know what's good for you!

Corpse Reviver (A Contessa Munroe Mystery #1)
A widowed Contessa flees to the northern waters in search of adventure. An entrepreneur dies on an ice pack excursion. But when the victim starts moonlighting from his locked cabin, can the Contessa uncover the true mystery of his death?

Catriona Cullodena Munroe, widow of the late Count de Los Palermo, has fled the family home, avoiding the scramble for title and land. As she searches for the life she always wanted, the Contessa, in the company of the autistic and rejected Tiff, must solve the mystery of a man who just won't let his business go.

Corpse Reviver is the first murder mystery involving the formidable and sometimes downright rude lady of leisure and her straight talking niece. Bonded by blood, and thrown together by fate, join this pair of thrill seekers as they realise that flirting with danger brings a price to pay.

When no one else takes charge, the cream must rise to the top!

Highlands and Islands Detective Thriller Series

https://grjordan.com/product/waters-edge

Join stalwart DI Macleod and his burgeoning new DC McGrath as they look into the darker side of the stunningly scenic and wilder parts of the north of Scotland. From the Black Isle to Lewis, from Mull to Harris and across to the small Isles, the Uists and Barra, this mismatched pairing follow murders, thieves and vengeful victims in an effort to restore tranquillity to the remoter parts of the land.

Be part of this tale of a surprise partnership amidst the foulest deeds and darkest souls who stalk this peaceful and most beautiful of lands, and you'll never see the Highlands the same way again

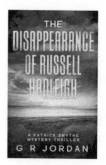

The Disappearance of Russell Hadleigh (Patrick Smythe Book 1)

https://grjordan.com/product/the-disappearance-of-russell-hadleigh

A retired judge fails to meet his golf partner. His wife calls for help while running a fantasy play ring. When Russians start co-opting into a fairly-traded clothing brand, can Paddy untangle the strands before the bodies start littering the golf course?

In his first full novel, Patrick Smythe, the single-armed former policeman, must infiltrate the golfing social scene to discover the fate of his client's husband. Assisted by a young starlet of the greens, Paddy tries to understand just who bears a grudge and who likes to play in the rough, culminating in a high stakes showdown where lives are hanging by the reaction of a moment. If you love pacey action, suspicious motives and devious characters, then Paddy Smythe operates amongst your kind of people.

Love is a matter of taste but money always demands more of its suitor.

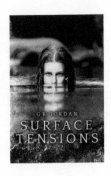

Surface Tensions (Island Adventures Book 1)
https://grjordan.com/product/surface-tensions
Mermaids sighted near a Scottish island. A town exploding in anger and distrust. And Donald's got to get the sexiest fish in town, back in the water.

"Surface Tensions" is the first story in a series of Island adventures from the pen of G R Jordan. If you love comic moments, cosy adventures and light fantasy action, then you'll love these tales with a twist. Get the book that amazon readers said, "perfectly captures life in the Scottish Hebrides" and that explores "human nature at its best and worst".

Something's stirring the water!

Lightning Source UK Ltd.
Milton Keynes UK
UKHW011142050721
386664UK00002B/789